If I Just Had Two Wings

If I Just Had Two Wings

Virginia Frances Schwartz

Fitzhenry & Whiteside

Published in Canada by Fitzhenry & Whiteside, 195 Allstate Parkway, Markham, Ontario L3R 4T8

Published in the United States by Fitzhenry & Whiteside, 121 Harvard Avenue, Suite 2, Allston, Massachusetts 02134

www.fitzhenry.ca   godwit@fitzhenry.ca

10 9 8 7 6 5 4 3 2

Fitzhenry & Whiteside acknowledges with thanks the Canada Council for the Arts, the Government of Canada through its Book Publishing Industry Development Program, and the Ontario Arts Council for their support in our publishing program.

National Library of Canada Cataloguing in Publication Data
Schwartz, Virginia Frances
If I just had two wings
ISBN 0-7737-3302-7 (bound) ISBN 0-7737-6192-6 (pbk.)
1. Underground railroad-Juvenile fiction.
2. Fugitive slaves-United States-Juvenile fiction. I. Title.
PS8587.C578613 2001   jC813'.6   C00-933350-9
PZ7.S4114If2001

U.S. Cataloging-in-Publication Data
(Library of Congress Standards)

Schwartz, Virginia Frances.
   If I just had two wings / Virginia Frances Schwartz.
  [228] p. : col. ill. ; cm.
Summary: Born on a plantation in Alabama, thirteen-year-old Phoebe has always dreamed of leaving her life as a slave. While picking cotton she learns of a way to escape to the north, and so begins her treacherous flight to Canada.
ISBN 0-7737-3302-7
ISBN 0-7737-6192-6 (pbk.)
1. Slavery - United States — Fiction.2. Underground railroad — Fiction. I. Title.
  [F] 21   2001

Printed in Canada

For my husband, Neil,
who makes the books possible.

PART ONE

---◇---

ON THE PLANTATION
SUMMER 1861

If I just had two wings,
Bright angels above,
I would fly away to the kingdom,
Bright angels above.

---◇---

CHAPTER
ONE

Phoebe's Dream

Phoebe was dark as a shadow and just as silent on that scorching July Alabama morning. She pinched wisps of cotton carefully from their dried boll shells, which cut into her fingers like a sharp razor blade.

Her thoughts kept drifting. Not long before, she had trailed behind her mother and her sister Rachel to Master Williams' big house, baking bread for the Master's supper, tasting stolen pieces of dough in the back kitchen. She worked side by side with the house slaves, their dresses crisp and starched, their voices soft and low. Bites of food all day long.

Like a dream world, remembered Phoebe.

She used to pretend her family lived in the big house. Come evening, all seven of them could sit around the oak table, eating from china plates until their bellies were full, their laughter ringing around the room. She would not have to go home to the silence of their cabin.

Only three of them lived there now. The others were gone. Rachel, the last to leave. To call up the past was to stir up ghosts.

Two months ago, after a hot spring, the south field of cotton came in too early. All the young slaves were needed in the field. Rachel stayed behind in the big house. She had trained five years to be a serving maid. She worked quickly, like her momma. But Phoebe hadn't had time to learn. The white overseer had shoved her out to the cotton fields, her dress wet with salt tears, two black braids tied tightly back against her smooth brown neck. Overnight she had to grow up.

"You gotta work on your own now." The overseer pointed to the acres of cotton fields behind the big house. "You're old enough to pick in the fields without your momma and your sister by your side."

He handed her the burlap sack she would wear each day across her shoulder to collect cotton. That first week, it carved a forever scar onto her bare flesh. At thirteen, she had learned not to feel the cut of the boll, but to squeeze back the tears and to bow her head low without meeting the overseer's eyes. Always.

Willow wisp girl, her father called her. Bone thin. Her huge eyes filled her face like two bright moons.

Out in the field, cotton branches waved so high above her head, she couldn't tell which way was home unless she squinted straight at the sun. That morning, she had filed in a long line with fifty other workers as they trudged to the field — men, women, and children, half asleep on their feet. She listened to the three field slaves picking nearest her, surrounded by row after row of sea-island cotton.

From across the row Emmett sang. Phoebe had known him since she was born. A bent, weatherbeaten man, he was as much a part of the plantation as the cotton fields and the sun. She loved how his back lifted straight up when he sang, making him look young again.

Oh free-dom! When I am free!
An' be-fo' I'd be a slave,
I'll be free-dom o-ver me!

"Freedom!" Liney fussed alongside Emmett. "It's what we're waitin' for, me and my children. You know anyone who might tell us how to get there?"

Liney plucked cotton with her strong brown arms. Beads of sweat sat on her forehead like pearls. At nineteen, Liney seemed a lifetime older than Phoebe. She was tall and lean with shining bronze muscles, slanted cinnamon eyes, and hair stretched flat into a bun. She had two babies but no husband when she arrived on the plantation a week ago, yet picked more cotton than any young man. Phoebe's mother warned her right away that Liney was a troublemaker, but Phoebe watched her closely whenever she could. She was full of secrets, someone who had lived a life somewhere beyond this plantation. She had seen things Phoebe might never see. If only she would tell her about them.

Beside Phoebe, Dianah pried loose a wad of cotton.

She was a string-bean-thin woman the color of molasses. Her dress hung on her like a loose sack.

"Gotta be the right time," she frowned. "If it's right, you just fly from here to there. If it's not, you might just as well be dead."

The overseer would check tonight to see if the plants were picked clean. Broken branches would kill the new-born cotton buds. He would sift through their sacks later at the mill for a stray piece of boll or leaf. Twenty-five lashes before you went to bed if the cotton wasn't clean, Dianah taught her. Until the overseer finished his check, slaves slept sitting straight up waiting for his return.

"I watch everyone who walks by," Liney said, eyeing the dirt road. "Wonder if they know the way out of here. Last night, I couldn't sleep listenin' for the hoot owl. I'm ready to run on the road."

She glanced over to the bushes where her children played, the shade cooling their bare skin. Sarah, her listening girl, was six years old with ink-black skin so slippery smooth, no one could grab her. She always watched over her little sister. Bethy was four years old but she had no baby fat. Both girls were small for their age. Since they were born, they had not been fed much meat. Plantation owners filled their tables with it every day, but most slaves only got one hog at Christmas to split among thirty families.

"You ain't never gonna find out by talkin'," Dianah scolded Liney. "Just like I always tell Jake." Jake was her son who was sold away to Master Watson at a neighboring plantation a month ago. Only on Saturday nights now did her sixteen-year-old boy come home to the Williams plantation to visit.

Phoebe smiled, remembering Jake. She had picked across from him for just a month before he left. He was so tall that in the mornings, he blocked out the sun with his body. She plucked cotton in the coolness his shadow cast over her. Sometimes, she looked up and noticed him staring at her. His eyes were the color of buckwheat honey and Phoebe had wanted to stare back, but couldn't. She could never tell when the overseer would ride past.

"Isn't he the one I heard last Saturday night complainin' about the overseer whippin' the slaves every day for no reason?" asked Liney. "He must want to know about the underground road, too."

"That boy can lead huntin' parties into the woods and predict when the weather will change, but all he dreams of is freedom," Emmett sighed.

"Too much talkin', too much dreamin'," muttered Dianah. "It just makes for trouble. Best if my boy keeps quiet. You, too, Liney."

"Talkin's the only way we'll find out about the underground railroad." Liney's voice cut across the rows into Phoebe's ears. "Some say the road's a crooked line that leads straight. Some say it's a secret road. But where do I find it around here?"

"Shush!"

Dianah nodded her head toward Phoebe, whose chocolate-brown eyes were fixed on the new slave. Liney was just six years older than the girl yet they were as different as night and day. Liney whisked her hands through the bushes, clean and quick, like a broom. She could talk all the while. She noticed everything, too. Where the overseer was hovering. What time it was by how high the sun had climbed. How many sacks each slave had picked. She could keep so many things in her head all at once.

Compared to Liney, Phoebe seemed spun from dreams and clouds. Her fingers touched the boll but did not pick. Her mind drifted. And since her sister's leave-taking, Phoebe had been at a standstill. She kept thinking about Rachel. Wondering where she was. She had begged her parents to tell her but they wouldn't. Forever looking across the field, expecting her to show up, but knowing that if she returned, she would not escape the Master's punishment.

"C'mon, girl!" Dianah called Phoebe from far off. "Cotton's waitin' to be picked!"

Phoebe sighed. Her mother, too, had prodded her like that in the kitchen of the big house. "Gotta pay attention, child. Master won't keep you if you don't work hard."

Phoebe forced her fingers to pluck cotton. Liney pressed her lips tightly together. The wind died down. The only sound was the scrape of fingers against the hard brown boll. The feather-soft cotton was trapped inside its thorny cage.

Once again Emmett's voice rose clear across the pure white cotton fields.

An' be-fo' I'd be a slave,
I'll be bur-ied in my grave.
Oh free-dom o-ver me!

When he finished singing, quiet once again brushed over the cotton fields. Phoebe looked at him from across the row, her face bright with questions.

"Who taught you to sing so fine, Emmett?"

"My daddy." Emmett grinned from ear to ear. "We been singin' in our family since we were born in Africa. Didn't stop when they dragged us out of there, either. Singin' kept my granddaddy alive aboard the slave ship to America."

Africa, Freedom Land, Phoebe's family called it. Across a wide, stormy ocean lay the land of the ancestors. They could never go back there.

"What was it like in your home in Africa?" she asked without thinking.

"Ain't just my family come from there, child. Yours too." Emmett turned his gray head toward Phoebe. "Over there, we were musicians to the king. Hunters. Herdsmen. Princesses and warriors. All that's long gone. Don't have nothin' now."

Dianah scowled. "Nothin' but work, you mean!"

"How did it happen, strong-workin' people like us, gettin' brought here?" Phoebe's hands were still, not picking anymore. The blisters on her fingers were raw and red.

"Guns. White slavetraders killed our king with 'em. My granddaddy and all the villagers ran down to the ocean to hide. Slave ships were waitin' there. If you didn't get on, they shot you dead. Someone pushed my granddaddy aboard."

"Took our names away when we landed here," Dianah spat. "Somehow we ain't people anymore. Call us slaves now."

"Our last name all be Williams like our Master." Emmett looked down at the dirt, the wrinkles in his face deeper than ever. "As if he's the king now. His dogs get better than us."

Phoebe was sorry she'd started Emmett talking. Whenever the old ones talked about the past, at first they'd be happy remembering but their words always ended in sorrow. She would never forget the story of how her great-great-granddaddy left Africa. He was traded by his own chief to the slavetraders for one barrel of rum. Tricked.

Phoebe decided Africa was full of black men's tears, just like here. Africa was not Freedom Land for her.

◈

That evening, Phoebe ate a supper of cold cornmeal cooked in bacon fat from the trough at the back of the barn. Fifty field workers dipped their bowls in beside her. Afterward, all the young ones scraped the trough clean with their fingers.

"Not enough to keep any fat on," her father complained to one of his friends. "Just enough to keep us alive."

Her father was the Master's blacksmith. White folks visited from miles around so he could shoe their horses or make them tools. He worked from dawn to dusk by a red-hot fire, a tall man with hard muscles that gleamed in the firelight. But in the last month, he had suddenly turned gray. That's how long it had been since Rachel, his fifteen-year-old daughter, had disappeared. He would not speak her name anymore. Most evenings he stared silently into the woods from the back porch.

The overseer rode past without a word. The check was over. It was safe to take her father's hand and walk to their cabin at the end of one of the slave rows, past the twenty wooden one-room shacks in five straight rows. Each cabin faced east so the slaves would awaken early with the morning light. The cabins had been hammered up quickly with rough-cut logs. Slanted roofs kept rain from soaking through. The windows had no glass so the air could come in.

Most cabins were brimful with babies but Phoebe was the last child at her home. Her brother, Isaac, and three sisters before him were all sold, scattered like leaves in a storm to plantations all over the South. Hannah and Jenny were sold off at auction, when Phoebe was a child. Isaac was traded for a high price. He knew blacksmithing, like his papa. Lucinda was bought by a slavetrader who loaded her into a wagon with ten other slaves. Phoebe would never forget that day. They tied Lucinda's wrists behind her back so she could not even wave goodbye. Phoebe had watched her disappear while her mother screamed, held back from running after the wagon by two strong white men.

Then, one morning last month, she awoke and the

space beside her was empty. Rachel was gone. Ever since she could remember, Phoebe had spent nearly every minute with Rachel. Running up and down the slave rows. Hand in hand, skipping to their chores. Side by side in the kitchen of the big house, until Phoebe was sent to the fields. *Rachel was beautiful*, thought Phoebe. *With long, wavy hair that had never been cut, hanging in two long braids to her waist. Taller than Papa.* She always wore a necklace of dried corn that their grandpa once made. He had dipped it in indigo, the color of the ocean in Africa. He said it was the color of his dreams.

Phoebe looked around the cabin. It was filled with a hush. Yet it echoed with ghosts. If she listened closely, she heard old memories. Lucinda whispering secrets in her ear. Rachel giggling in the dark beside her. Her brother Isaac racing her to the field, lifting her up and up until she was spinning high in the air. Gone-away things. Phoebe could not think of them without hanging her head down.

Phoebe swept the dirt floor clean with a hard wire broom. Cricket calls filled the darkening cabin. Now was time to ask.

"Momma, tell me, what is the underground railroad?"

"Hush, child!" Her mother's eyes popped wide open as if her daughter had said a forbidden word. "Where'd you hear about that?"

"Liney was talkin' in the fields today about goin' on it."

"It's a dangerous road!" Her voice rang shrilly in the girl's ears. "Liney's askin' for trouble! Stay away from her, you hear? Promise me now."

At bedtime, Phoebe looked out the window. Hundreds of stars filled the night sky like the hundreds of questions ringing in her mind. She covered herself with a burlap sack and curled up on the floor. When she shut her eyes, all she saw were rows and rows of sea-island cotton. She fell asleep. In her dream that night, she was twirling through the rows in a white cotton dress that blew around her legs like a breeze. As she danced, she lost all memory of being born a slave on a cotton plantation in Alabama. She just lifted up her feet and flew high above the white fields, light as air. Her dress blew around her like a cloud. She saw a single white star shining. Somewhere it was dawn.

She slept on.

C H A P T E R
T W O

Old Willie's Learning

The sun was just rising the next day when Phoebe trudged to the fields, her bare brown feet covered with dew. Already the air was heavy. She passed Old Willie's cabin. He was a midnight-black man, too old to work in the fields any longer. He minded the youngest children before they were sent off to pick cotton. He usually stood at the door come dawn, waving to the sleepy children on their way to the fields. But the doorway was empty now. He had been in bed three long days. He couldn't breathe when the weather was humid. Phoebe heard the rustling of pans inside and knew his wife, Annie Mae, was cooking breakfast for him. But no doctor came until you were sick a week. Master's rule. Old Willie had to wait.

"To see if you're strong enough to make it," Dianah had told her. "Then it's worth the price of a doctor comin' out."

As Phoebe walked on, she saw rows and rows of

cotton ahead. Each night as she closed her eyes, all she saw were acres of whiteness. She usually floated to sleep soon afterward. Suddenly Phoebe halted at the edge of the field, the workers passing her by. Last night, she remembered, she had fallen asleep thinking about the underground railroad. Liney's words had lit up her mind all that day. And then the dream had come. It had begun with dancing, but then somehow she was flying up in the air above the fields like a crow. The rows of cotton stretched out below her. *How did I get up there?* she wondered. *Did I have wings? Where was I going?*

Questions. She was always asking questions. It had begun with Old Willie. He made her wonder about everything. She remembered how Old Willie led her and all the young ones out to the pine woods at dusk years ago. They stood in a line facing the tall pines. Old Willie's words echoed like whispers in and out of the trees. Several children hung back, sucking their thumbs. But eight-year-old Phoebe stared wide-eyed straight to where Willie pointed.

"Listen! I'm gonna teach you a signal our people gotta know."

They all listened, brown eyes watching. Phoebe's small hand rested in Willie's old wrinkled one.

"Whoo! Whoo! Whoo!" called a hoot owl from the pines.

Silence. A deep, thinking silence.

Then "Whoo! Whoo! Whoo!" echoed from deeper in the woods, as if they rose up from inside an empty rain barrel.

Phoebe studied Old Willie as he cupped his hands to his mouth and bent his head low.

"Whoo! Whoo! Whoo!" he sang to the owls. Short notes that lingered on the air long afterward.

The owls always answered him.

"Whoo! Whoo! Whoo!"

"Now you do it," he coaxed one child.

"Who? Who? Who?" The calls came like questions from the child, not like the hoots of an owl. One by one, the other children tried. The owls never answered back.

"You be the one. You can do it, Phoebe." Old Willie pushed Phoebe ahead of him so that all she could see on every side of her were the pine woods where the invisible owls lived. She took a deep breath.

"Whoo! Whoo! Whoo!" Her voice rang out deeply and loudly.

They all listened, silently in a row, the young children and the old man.

"Whoo! Whoo! Whoo!" an owl answered her.

Old Willie nodded his white head and smiled. He slipped a cornhusk doll into Phoebe's hand. It was yellowed and dry with shreds of burlap for arms spreading away from its body like wings.

"I made this for the child who learns best. That signal may save your life one day. Be a conductor callin' you, soundin' like an owl so no white man's gonna catch on. An owl's gonna spread its wings if it hears you come by. But a friend will stay put and help."

"Where's it callin' me to?" She spun the doll in the air.

"Fly to freedom, girl," Old Willie whispered in her ear.

She had heard that word before. *Freedom*. A deep-sounding word that dropped like a stone from her father's lips as if it was something that could never be reached. A place far away as heaven. Another gone-away thing.

"If it's takin' us to freedom, why haven't you gone there yourself?" she fired back at him.

"Ain't you a sassy one!" Old Willie grinned so wide, Phoebe could see gums where his teeth once were. "It was where I once thought I was goin' but I can't get there now. You gotta run day and night to reach it."

He patted his left leg, thinner than the right one, always trailing behind him. "Born that way. Lungs ain't strong, either. But sittin' still like I do, I hear a lot. I learn secrets. That's why I'm pushin' you on to freedom, girl. You got those long, skinny legs forever runnin'. You gonna make it to freedom."

A boy named Samuel yanked Old Willie's sleeve. "What's freedom?"

"Freedom is laying your head down at night, knowing the next day is yours. But here, every inch of us, head to toe, belongs to someone else," he shook his head sadly.

◈

All that day, Phoebe picked slowly. Dianah constantly reminded her to keep her mind on the cotton. The overseer had flicked his whip beside her, too, slicing a cut onto her arm. It had startled her and set her to picking faster, but nothing stopped her from remembering Old Willie's words. His voice ran through her mind. "You got those long, skinny legs forever runnin'. You gonna make it to freedom."

Late that night, when Phoebe curled up on her sleeping mat in the dark cabin, she reached out for the cornhusk doll lying next to her. It was faded now and its wings were shredded. But she still kept it by her mat and hugged it goodnight each night. She had told her family that Old Willie had given it to her, but she didn't say why. She didn't dare speak the word *freedom* aloud. Not even to Rachel. Since that time with Old Willie, she had gone to work, first at the big house and now in the fields. She never had any more of his learning to think about again. She had been afraid at times that she would grow up to be like Old Willie, looking all his life at what he wanted somewhere just on the other side of the field, but never getting there. *No,* she reminded herself, squeezing the cornhusk doll. *A dream has come to me, filling me brimful with light. I have never felt this way. Before, just sorrows came to me. Now I see something far away. If only I could see it clearer. Willie said all the young ones have a chance to make it to freedom. Freedom must be the place I'm dreamin' about! But what is freedom?*

Old Willie had said the Williamses were free. Once, from the back kitchen window of the big house when she should have been stirring mint julep to cool it, Phoebe had spied their two young daughters, Charlotte and Pauline, playing on the lawn. They were dressed in frilly pink dresses and their hair was combed smooth and tied up in shiny ribbons. So pretty and cool, they did not have to work in the fields. She would have liked one of their fancy dresses instead of those she wore — one of burlap, the other a torn pillowcase. *No matter*, she sighed. But she wanted to run in to her momma whenever she pleased and skip up the pine staircase of the plantation house as they did or maybe fly on the swing in their backyard with Rachel.

She just had to look at her sister to know what she was thinking. Her chestnut eyes sparkled with fun. In a flash, Rachel would have dashed out to the yard to play if it was allowed. For a moment, she thought she heard Rachel calling her in a loud, clear voice. *Phoebe! Come with me!* Tears sprang to Phoebe's eyes immediately. Then her mouth set in a straight line. She yanked herself from her daydream. *Rachel's not here. She went somewhere without me. She didn't even tell me where. I have to be a field slave now. I can't be seen by the big house. I can't have my momma by my side anymore. But I want something else. A place where I won't have to pick cotton or bow my head before any white man like I was invisible. I'll be free and not a slave anymore. But where is it? Somewhere I have to run to, that's what Liney says. And how far beyond the Williamses' must I travel before I get there?*

When Phoebe got thinking this way, she could almost stamp her feet on the ground she was in such a hurry to run to the freedom place Old Willie was talking about. It wasn't a fancy dress she wanted. It was something Charlotte and Pauline were born with that she didn't have. Without it, it was just as if she were born with a bad leg like Old Willie, looking far off to the freedom place but having both feet chained down to plantation ground.

C H A P T E R
T H R E E

The Color Red

On the second day of heat, word came that Master Williams was worried about his cotton. Cotton loved sun but not a heat wave. Heat could dry it up so it wouldn't even be good enough to stuff pillows with.

The white overseer was already perched on his horse in the cotton fields when Phoebe arrived, a whip hanging from his belt. "Move it! Master says bring in twice the cotton you picked yesterday or there won't be no Sunday break. Get this cotton in before the sun kills it." He galloped off in a cloud of smoke.

Sunday break! How Phoebe waited for the week to end. First came Saturday night outside the barn, the moon lighting up everyone's face. Banjo notes cutting the warm air. Dancing in the dark. Women's skirts flying. Laughter like cannon booms from the men, even her father, who'd been storing it up inside himself all week. Teenagers high jumping. Dianah's son, Jake, always the winner, a victory smile flashing across his face, catching her eye, making her smile, too. Phoebe remembered how once Jake had brushed past her, grabbed her hand, and twirled her in circles like Isaac used to do. She had shut her eyes and spun, as light as sea-island cotton, on tiptoe at first. Then, breathless, she felt her feet circle above the earth as Jake lifted her up. Her head still spun and her heart pumped long after he set her down.

On that one night, the slaves went to bed late and awakened to Sunday church and Emmett singing. But, all week, there was work to be done. Every full-grown slave was expected to pick two hundred pounds of cotton a day. The old and the young picked less. Phoebe was lucky if she could pick eighty pounds. Cotton slipped between her fingers like water. She had her mind on other things. All day, Phoebe pictured herself flying high above the field. She heard a powerful flapping in her ears, cool wind blowing against her face, and then Dianah interrupted her.

"That Phoebe's dreamin' about something again. Wake up, girl, and pick!"

"He gotta be either jokin' or crazy to pick that much cotton in this heat." Emmett swatted a fly away from his head. "I picked my fill yesterday. They need to bring some more young men out here to help."

"Overseer don't joke with nobody," muttered Dianah.

But Liney's hands whizzed over the cotton so fast that Phoebe could just see a blur of brown arm and muscle. Over and over again, she filled the sacks brimful with feather-soft cotton.

By noon, all the sacks the overseer had left were stuffed. The workers squatted in the thin shade of the cotton plants. From hand to hand, they passed around a gourd shell dipped in water and corn cakes that crumbled if they didn't eat them fast enough. Bethy crawled onto Liney's lap but her sister dragged her off. She wiggled like a worm out of Sarah's arms. They both spilled over Emmett, then all three tumbled onto Liney's lap. Emmett looked up, startled. For the first time since Phoebe met her, Liney laughed, her teeth flashing white against her bronze face. She reminded Phoebe of an African princess Emmett once told her about, with a crown of sun instead of jewels. She was strong enough to carry the sun on her head without getting burned.

Heat waves rose from the ground to the air, shimmering. The soft ripple of the children's giggles was the only sound in the field. A field of hot still air. Noontime. Phoebe's eyes shut. For ten minutes everyone lay down upon the ground and rested. Their thoughts drifted up to the sky like slow white clouds sailing by.

Liney stretched out her long legs. Some days she talked, unpacking the stories in her mind like pulling memories out of an old chest.

"Back in Africa, Angolans wore animal hides. They never saw cloth before," she began one story. "And such a color, too. Bright red! I never liked that color. It's bad luck. Blood color. Trick color. That's how the traders got 'em."

"Got who, Liney?" Phoebe sat up to listen.

"All my family's village a hundred years ago.

Slavetraders dropped pieces of red cloth on the ground in my great-grandma's village, makin' a long trail out to the ocean. All the women grabbed it. Wondrous! they thought. Men, too, came runnin' after the red cloth. Ran aboard the slaveship to touch it."

Phoebe took a deep breath and held it in, waiting.

"When everyone was onboard, they were chained down. Trapped below in the galley. That ship sailed off to America."

"One moment they were free just like white folks and the next — slaves," sighed Dianah. "No turnin' back."

"That color tricked 'em." Liney spat on the ground as if her words tasted sour. "I wouldn't be sittin' here if not for that red cloth. I'd be livin' in freedom instead of always lookin' for it."

Phoebe wrapped her arms around her legs and rocked back and forth. Tears sat at the edge of her eyes. *Stories. Sorrows. They weigh us down. Each of us has a past we wish never happened. Dragged out of Africa. Torn apart from our families. No better here. I wonder what sorrow has made Liney so restless to run on the underground road.* The only stories she could trade with Liney were about her sold-away brother and sisters and the one sister, Rachel, who had disappeared. Her throat jammed up whenever she tried to talk to her momma about it. She could not tell it to this new girl yet. Her momma had told her not to trust Liney. One evening, as they had walked home together from the fields, they'd passed by Phoebe's cabin. Her mother stood in the doorway, staring out, frowning at the new girl. Liney walked on, without a wave. She did not say goodnight to Phoebe as she always did. Phoebe had wanted to run after Liney, but dared not.

Beside her now, she felt Liney stiffen just like that night. From across the field, they spied a tunnel of smoke rolling toward them. Fast.

"Leave him to me." Liney stood up, casting a long shadow over the field as if to hide them all.

The overseer dismounted his horse.

"How much did you pick?" he sneered at her.

"We all picked as fast as we could, like you told us."

"How much did the old man pick?"

Emmett opened his mouth to answer but Liney spoke too fast for him. "Plenty! He may look skinny but he's keepin' up with us."

"Get up now! Got more bags need fillin'. No more breaks!" He flung two hundred burlap sacks down at their feet.

The afternoon sun was hotter than ever before. It shone through Phoebe's headscarf, making her dizzy. She held one hand over her eyes to hide from the sun, picking with the other hand. Liney splashed drops of water from the gourd shell over Phoebe's face.

"Cool you off some, child," offered Liney. "Lie down under the plants for a spell with my children. Sleep 'til I call you."

Liney's voice soothed her like a cool breeze. She watched over her just as her sister Rachel always had. Phoebe crawled under the plants where Bethy was curled up, her cornrows undone and soaked with sweat. She had big gingersnap eyes the color of sugar cookies Phoebe had seen once in the kitchen of the big house yet never tasted. When she smiled at Phoebe, it was like a ray of sun peeking through on a cloudy day. Phoebe couldn't resist twisting her hair into neat braids and rocking her to sleep. Bethy was as light in her arms as a half-filled sack of cotton.

Phoebe remembered how Rachel used to rock her, her back against the warmth of her sister's chest, Rachel humming a lullaby into her ears. Phoebe's throat choked up. *Did Rachel hold onto me and feel as I do, that this child does not know what is ahead of her? That there is no escape for her? That no matter how much her momma loves her, still, it is not enough?*

All the while Phoebe watched Liney bend low, her long arms stretching out, fingers dancing over the cotton.

"How do you do it, Liney?" Dianah shook her head. "All day long, you just workin' and workin'. Pickin' your share and our share, too. You gonna be wore out by supper!"

"No matter. Gotta keep busy. Stay out of trouble that way."

"I wish I was a young man again," joked Emmett. "I could pull in so much cotton, I'd save you all some work. You could just sleep under the cotton branches all day long while I picked."

Their voices floated away. Phoebe heard only the high ring of the women's laughter as she drifted off to sleep in the cool shade of the cotton plants. She stretched out and smiled. Soon she was dancing in a white cotton dress, smooth and shiny as a pearl, blowing in the breeze.

There was a great flapping sound all around her. Suddenly, the field workers were below her and she was lifting up and up. She was sure she had wings this time and she pumped them hard as she could to get away. Beside her flew someone with a crown so bright, it blinded her. Far below her, the cotton fields sizzled, but where she was flying, the sun grew dimmer. Day turned to dark. She beat her wings harder and harder to stay up in the air. She flew to a dreamplace where there was no cotton, no slaves, and no sun anymore.

CHAPTER
FOUR

Losing Liney

For seven days, the sun rose high in the sky, burning everything crisp brown. The ground split into long, dry cracks like the lines in an old person's face. Cotton withered inside the boll faster than it could be picked. From the nearby rows, Phoebe heard the field workers groan. Sometimes a picker far off would start a song and the others would sing back to them. One loud voice calling. A chorus answering it. But not one of them sang that week. It was hard to even breathe. Liney filled hundreds of sacks and swore to the overseer that Emmett and Phoebe were picking fast. By the day's end, all the field slaves stumbled back to their cabins, drenched in sweat.

On the eighth day, while Phoebe drew water from the well behind the Master's mansion, the sound of male voices drifted to her ears. She froze in her tracks. The overseer and Master Williams were speaking with

Master Watson on the lawn. She shrank back behind a tree, remembering that field slaves shouldn't be seen near the house. Their sharp voices sliced into her mind like a knife.

"You'll sure get you a fine pickin' girl," bragged the overseer to Master Watson. "Every day, I hide out in the fields and study Liney at work. She picks faster than any slave I know."

"What price are you askin' for her?" Master Watson questioned.

"If you're willin' to pay one thousand for her, Watson," Master Williams waved his cigar in the air, "she's yours."

Phoebe bit her fingers hard to keep from screaming out.

"This war's been sendin' slave prices sky high!" complained Master Watson. "If that fool Lincoln doesn't stop fightin', we are going to be in deep trouble here in the South."

Master Williams wiped his mouth clean of cigar flakes and laughed. His gold teeth flashed in the noonday sun.

"Don't you worry any about this war. Had some squabbles over the last few months but . . . it'll be over by Sunday dinner. Then we can all raise cotton prices and get rich."

"If Liney works like you say, she's worth it." Master Watson and Master Williams shook hands. "Send her to me tomorrow morning at dawn. Keep her babies. I don't want 'em."

Phoebe shot out from that tree past the Confederate jasmine vines that lined the backyard, their white perfumed petals spilling all over the ground. She bent lower than the bushes and flew to the field, darker than a shadow and just as quick.

"Girl, you look like you swallowed too much water. What's wrong?" Dianah grabbed the bucket from Phoebe's trembling hands.

Phoebe's heart pounded wildly, filling her with something she did not wish to know. But the words came anyway. *To be a slave is to be nobody. We can be bought and sold like animals.* Phoebe felt Liney's hand touch hers. She recalled all the times Liney looked out for her, picking both their shares, letting her sleep in the hot afternoons. She had felt like a child beside the older girl. Phoebe's words broke loose like a midsummer thunderstorm.

"They . . . speakin' about you up at the house," she said, grabbing Liney's hands. "Master just sold you to Master Watson 'cause you pickin' so fast!"

Phoebe caught her breath. Liney stood still, her arms hanging stiffly at her sides. Phoebe had never seen her look like that before. All her brightness dimmed.

"When am I goin'?" Liney's words dropped like stones sinking into well water, sinking down and far away.

"Tomorrow morning at dawn . . ." Phoebe hesitated. She did not want to go on but Liney must know everything. "And he said . . . he don't want your babies."

Liney shot a quick look at her children playing. They chased each other around a cotton plant, dressed in burlap shorts. Their laughter rippled on the wind. They had not heard. Liney walked into the field with her back to everyone and stared into the endless rows of cotton.

"What are we gonna do?" Phoebe tugged hard on Dianah's arm.

"Shush!" hissed Dianah between clenched teeth. "Ain't nothin' can be done now. Ought never to have told her. Let's pick!"

I had to warn her! Give her a chance to get away, Phoebe pouted. Liney stood straight-backed in the field, taller than Phoebe ever remembered her. Phoebe picked as fast as she could to make up for all the times Liney picked for her. When Liney returned to the bushes, once again her fingers flew over the cotton.

"He made up my mind, that Master Watson," said Liney. "I gotta go, one way or the other."

All Phoebe wanted was to yank Liney to safety. She looked in all directions. There was no place to hide, just acres of cotton all around.

"What you gonna do, Liney?" she begged from across the row.

Liney looked up for just a second, long enough for Phoebe to see her cinnamon eyes darken with secrets.

"Just what I have to, girl. Just what I have to."

Phoebe swallowed hard. She had known Liney just one month yet wished to hold onto her. Since Rachel left, she had no one to talk to. No one to call a friend. The Master would sell Liney away like Isaac and her sisters. Liney would be another gone-away thing. Phoebe hung her head down. Tears spilled onto her burlap dress.

Emmett's voice journeyed low and deep across the field toward them.

Oh, way down yon-der by my-self,
I could-n't hear no-bo-dy pray.
In the val-ley on my knees,
I could-n't hear no-bo-dy pray.

A hush of silence brushed over the hot field as every-one listened to his words rise high above the rows of cotton, up and up into the wide blue sky.

C H A P T E R
F I V E

Running With the Moon

Phoebe lay in bed that night listening. A hoot owl screeched from the back woods. "Whoo! Whoo! Whoo!" She sat up as it called again, farther and farther away. "Whoo! Whoo! Who . . ." Then a silence hung suspended over the back porches. Phoebe tossed in her sleep. Her shoulders ached from the cutting weight of the sack.

The wild barking of bloodhounds awoke her sometime before dawn. One by one, slave families slipped outside onto their back porches. Lanterns flashed in the back woods. Men yelled. The woods shook with the pounding of feet. Then the song began.

Even in the darkness, she knew the voice, bittersweet and slow, a voice from her childhood.

Wade in the wat-er, chil-dren.
Wade in the wat-er.
God's gon-na trou-ble the wa-ter.

Emmett sang deep and clear. All around them, slave voices rose up. Women and men, half asleep. Here and there, a few children. Phoebe got up and went out to the back porch. Her father stood tall, singing along with Emmett. His overalls hung on him like an empty sack that needed filling.

"She couldn't wait no longer," he sighed. "Slavecatchers on her trail. That full moon's gonna light up the ground too much."

"Who's out there, Papa?" The words came out of Phoebe's mouth even though she knew the answer.

He put his arm around his daughter's shoulder and looked at his wife. Phoebe's mother nodded, her face stern and dark in the moonlight.

"It's Liney lookin' for the road. She's tryin' to get to freedom. They must've checked her cabin and found her gone. Emmett's singin' to warn her to walk in the water to cover her trail from the hounds."

"Where is freedom?" Phoebe asked. She glanced quickly at her mother before going on. "Is it . . . is it the underground railroad?"

"Freedom is north, where your grandpa always dreamed of going. He believed Canada was promised land. 'Someday one of us is gonna get to it,' he said. 'No slaves there.' I hear we can own land. Not like this. We got nothin' here. Don't even own our families . . ."

He stared, misty-eyed, at something Phoebe could not see.

"Dreamin' leads to trouble," her mother interrupted. "Gotta put your mind on the here and now. Phoebe drifts off enough, already."

But her papa shook his head.

"Gotta have dreams to see you through. Get lost without 'em. My father had 'em. Liney must have had a dream, too."

"Why don't we go off?" Phoebe tugged her mother's sleeve.

"Not safe, child." She shook her head. "You need a conductor. They pick you. See you are ready. Teach you the secret way to go. They may run with you or stay behind to help others. Only they know the way."

"You gotta want to go so bad you run like a rabbit hundreds of miles with nothin' on your mind but freedom and no food in your belly," her father added.

"How could Liney take Sarah and Bethy, then?" asked Phoebe.

"She didn't. Folks told her not to. Slow her down too much. Not safe for a family." The lines in her father's forehead were deep and pressed like scars onto Phoebe's heart. "Those hounds tear you apart and that ain't nothin' to what the overseer will do. Gotta stay put."

Phoebe remembered Emmett singing, "I could-n't hear no-bo-dy pray" all last evening around Liney's door. He tried to warn her not to go. Nobody around to help her, said the song, nobody around to pray for her. Phoebe had wished for a safe place to hide Liney. There was none on this plantation. She leaned across the porch, so many words aching in her throat.

How could Liney know about the secret ways if nobody was around to help her? Did she just up and run on her own? Or did she meet a conductor? She told some of the slaves she was goin'. Must have wanted them to look out for her children. But why didn't she tell me? I wish she thought I was her friend. She didn't say goodbye, same as Rachel. Why would they both do that? Did they think I was still a child who would whisper away their plans? Or did they both go to some secret place that they were afraid to tell anyone about?

Answers leaped in Phoebe's mind like pieces of a puzzle finally fitting together.

"Liney didn't tell me she was leavin'," she spoke up. "No goodbyes. Just like Rachel."

Phoebe saw her mother turn toward her father with sharp eyes. They were both silent.

"She's gotta know now. It's time. She won't tell," she heard her father finally say.

"Rachel couldn't leave no sign," her mother sighed. "She ran off. Had to."

"Where did she go?"

"On the underground, like Liney," explained her father. "She heard up at the big house that the Master was plannin' to use her to breed more slaves. Rachel would have no part of it. She left with Samuel from the next cabin."

Phoebe remembered once seeing Rachel and Samuel, walking hand in hand, her sister beaming bright as the sun. They had quickly dropped their hands when they noticed her. It was only now Phoebe realized Sam had disappeared, too. Slaves came and went on the plantation all the time. She thought he'd been hired out somewhere. He was a good hunter, like Jake. He tended the foxhounds on the plantation, preparing them for the chase. *But they didn't tell me about Rachel!*

She could not stop from screaming out, "You never told me! You refused to say her name. All I wanted was to know what happened to her."

Her father swallowed hard. He tightened his arm around her shoulders. Phoebe's tears spilled onto his bare chest.

"It was a hurtin' thing to see her go. Nearly all my children gone. And nothin' I could do to help."

"All we got left is you." Phoebe felt her mother's warm hand touch her back. "I'm about to lose my mind, not knowin' how to keep you safe."

"Once my daddy dreamed of runnin', too. But now, we gotta hold fast 'til the war's over. If Lincoln wins, maybe he'll set us all free," her father said.

"This war's just started." Her mother sighed again. "Gonna be a long time before it's all over and done with."

The families turned back inside their cabins but they did not sleep. One by one, they prayed for clouds to cover the bright moon. They prayed for it to rain so hard, it'd cover up Liney's tracks. Phoebe shut her eyes and called the girl's name over and over. *Liney. Liney. Liney.* It sounded like a prayer, too.

C H A P T E R
S I X

Ghost Woman

No rain fell that night. Morning came too soon with hazy skies and still, hot air that pressed down on Old Willie's chest like a flat iron. He sat propped up in bed as Phoebe passed by with the workers on her way to the fields. He did not wave. When the doctor had finally come, there had been nothing he could do.

The millions of questions in Phoebe's mind were hushed. All that morning, she picked silently, head down. The overseer was nowhere to be seen. Emmett did not sing. Liney's children did not come to the fields. The only sound was the scrape of brown hands against the dry boll. Cicadas chirped across the cotton field. Sssh! . . . Sssh! . . . Sssh! . . . They whirred through the heat-heavy air.

At noon, men on horseback rode toward them. A lone horse trailed behind with a load on its back. A pack of barking hounds followed.

"Keep your head down!" warned Dianah. "Keep workin'!"

Phoebe felt the pounding of horse hooves shake the ground beneath her feet. She kept her eyes down. *What if they ask me where Liney is?* she worried. *No wonder my momma didn't want to tell me about the underground railroad.*

Sacks tumbled down at her feet.

"Fill these by the time I get back or else." The overseer's order snapped like thunder across the field into her ears.

Phoebe jumped back. Lying belly down across the back of a horse was Liney. She was tied with thick ropes but her long legs and arms flapped in all directions. Blood poured from her mouth. The hounds had ripped her legs so bad, they were raw red instead of strong and brown. Blood red. Through the back of Liney's torn dress, Phoebe could see rows and rows of angry red welts. Whip burns. Phoebe felt them throb just as if they were carved on her own flesh. But worst of all was how Liney stared at the ground, eyes wide open, not seeing her.

Ghost woman.

Phoebe's stomach heaved. She felt as though she was going to be sick. *My friend! I never had the chance to call you that. Never had the chance to help you, like you helped me. And I'll never get to tell Rachel what she meant to me, either. I have no way of knowing if she's alive. It could be her, lying on that horse. Look what they can do to us! Tear us to pieces and feed us to the hounds! Nothin' is left of you, Liney. You may not live 'til nightfall.*

"Sure is a shame," sighed Emmett after the overseer rode off. "Strong girl like Liney hurtin' so bad."

"That girl just couldn't wait to go." Dianah nodded her head toward Phoebe. "Better pick or we're all gonna get in trouble."

Let her mend, prayed Phoebe. *Let them forget what she has done. Give her back to Bethy and Sarah and me.*

The three workers picked all day in a hazy daydream. Their arms yanked cotton from the bushes into their sacks. They chewed silently on corn cakes as they worked without sitting down. They passed a jug of water around without one word. All they thought about was Liney.

At dusk dark, the voice of the overseer broke the spell as he rode onto the field. All their sacks were not filled yet. The other field workers had picked their fill, and had already headed home, but not them.

"Can't keep up now, can you?" His whip slapped the back of Emmett's swollen heel hard. Ten stinging slaps.

The whip struck Phoebe next, wrapping itself around her bare neck. She leaped high and scurried into the woods where the horse couldn't follow. Behind her, she heard Dianah scream as the whip cut across her dark brown cheek.

Phoebe returned to an empty cabin. No supper waited. She munched on a summer apple wondering where her parents were. Her whip burns throbbed. She had never felt so alone before. There was no one to talk to. Not her papa or her momma, not even Liney anymore. When she thought of Liney, a picture flashed in her mind. Liney with the sun shining all around her, wearing a crown so bright, it blinded her. With a jolt, Phoebe remembered something from her dream. She had not been alone. She traveled with someone whose crown shone like the sun. *Liney! Where are you? We're supposed to be together!*

Suddenly the cabin seemed too small. She burst out the door and ran straight toward the back of one of the slave rows. On the front step of Liney's cabin sat Emmett, his gray head sunk in his hands. He looked up when he heard her and shook his head.

"No use, girl. She's not here."

His words slapped her like a whip.

"Wh . . . where's Liney at?"

"Annie Mae took her off somewhere. Master says he don't want anyone near Liney. Your parents went to help. I hear she's sleepin' deep. Needs herbs and healin' now."

"Will she live?"

"Sure hope so. Got those two young ones waitin' on her."

Emmett nodded at Liney's cabin. Phoebe stepped toward the door but Emmett's hand shot out to stop her.

"They scared, girl. Tried to feed 'em but they not talkin' and not eatin' both. Ran away from me like I was a bee gonna sting 'em." He held out two corn pones.

Phoebe lifted them out of his hand.

"Go on rest now, Emmett. I'll feed 'em."

Inside the cabin, it was dark and quiet. In a far corner, Phoebe saw the small bundle of Bethy on the floor and Sarah sitting up beside her. Phoebe stepped nearer. Bethy was asleep on Sarah's lap, her head soaked with tears.

"You doin' good, Sarah," Phoebe whispered. "Carin' for your sister. Your momma would be proud."

Sarah stiffened against the wall when she heard Phoebe. Her face was thin and dirty. She looked like she had not slept since Liney ran.

Phoebe went on. "I once had four sisters. Did I ever tell you that?" Sarah shook her head. "You remind me of my Rachel. Two years older than me, just like you and Bethy. Always watchin' out for me. That's what big sisters do."

A long pause. Sarah sat up straight, listening.

"I saw your momma today."

Inch by inch, Sarah leaned toward Phoebe. Bethy did not stir.

"She was in the fields, child. She came back to us."

"But . . . where is she? We've been waitin' and waitin' on her!"

"She's plumb tired. Had a long trip. Sleepin' deep now."

"Did she ask for us?"

"She begged Emmett, 'Bring food to my girls,' and she say to me, 'Feed my girls.' You gonna let me do as she says?"

Phoebe held out a corn pone and slipped it into Sarah's open mouth.

"Good girl. Your momma's comin' back soon. You're gonna go to the fields every day with me and Emmett 'til she's better. I'll fetch you come morning."

Phoebe held the other corn pone out and nodded her head toward Bethy. Sarah woke her and held the food to her mouth. The child yawned and chewed it with her eyes shut. Once again, she fell asleep, leaning on her big sister.

Sarah lay her head on Phoebe's lap, pulling her sister with her. As Phoebe stroked Sarah's hair, huge tears fell down the child's face. Her body shook with sobs. Phoebe waited until deep dark, until Sarah finally slept. She ran home then and had just stepped inside her cabin when she heard her parents' footsteps on the path.

"Why are you still awake?" demanded her mother. "Tomorrow's a long day and that overseer will be watchin' for sure."

Phoebe stood tall before her parents for the first time.

"You been with Liney. I gotta know how she is."

"Bleedin' from everywhere. Mighty weak," her father sighed. "There's a split clear through the middle of her tongue. She can't talk to nobody about the road now. Master fixed that. No one's ever gonna know how they hurt Liney."

Phoebe squeezed the cornhusk doll tightly in her pocket. "Will she live?"

"Liney's tough. If she wants to pull through, she will."

"Master says anyone hangin' around Liney will be punished," her mother instructed. "Don't visit her! Hear?"

Then her mother's look softened. She pulled Phoebe closer and touched the whip burns on her neck. She greased the burns and smoothed the blisters on her fingers. Her touch was always gentle and usually set Phoebe to dreaminess. But not that night. Her parents soon fell asleep but Phoebe lay awake long hours. When she shut her eyes, she saw Liney stretched out on the horse. She seemed as far away as her sold-away sisters.

Suddenly a picture flashed in her mind. She remembered sneaking to the auction when Hannah and Jenny were sold. She had probably been about five years old then. She had run there with Rachel, who had squeezed her hand hard the whole while. White Masters bid for them. Phoebe began to pray silently. *Keep them here. Keep them safe.* The hammer banged down, making Phoebe jump. Hannah was yanked from the platform first, then Jenny. Pushed into wagons headed in different directions. She did not even know which way to look. Phoebe had blinked a moment and her sisters had vanished forever.

Tears poured down Phoebe's face. She had never been allowed to cry for her sisters. Her momma would shush her if she did. She had hidden her tears in a dark corner of their cabin just like Sarah. But she could not hold them in any longer. *I can't lose another person! Bring Hannah and Jenny back! Bring my all my sisters back! Bring Isaac back! Bring Liney back!* She pounded the dirt floor with both fists and both feet. She saw the Master's face and beat the floor harder. After a long while, she sat up and wiped her face dry.

This all happened because Liney had to make plans in a hurry. How bad do I want to go? Just as bad as Liney but I don't want to ever get caught. I can plan my way. I can wait 'til I'm ready, 'til my time comes and I know it.

In the dark night, Dianah's words jumped in her mind like lightning sparks. "If it's right, you just fly from here to there."

The One I'm Learning

Next morning, all was quiet and dark inside Old Willie's cabin. A torn potato sack covered his window to block the sun. Phoebe glanced at the empty doorway as she passed by with the other slaves. Her stomach tightened into a fist. On her shoulder, Bethy lay asleep. Sarah held her hand, squeezing her lips together, checking in all directions for a sign of her mother. Out in the field with acres of cotton surrounding them and sun blasting down, there was nothing Phoebe could do to make anyone feel better. Emmett limped slower than ever today, his feet swollen like two tree stumps. Dianah picked steadily but didn't talk. The girls sat in the shade silently. They did not play. A spell lay upon them as thick as summer haze.

The overseer eyed them from the dirt road. Phoebe could almost hear his thoughts travel across the field. "What are you all gonna do now, without Liney?"

There was only one thing Phoebe thought she could do. *Something to make time move. Something to break the spell. I can pick fast for Liney*, she decided. *I'll pretend she's here beside me pickin', as if her strong arms are pullin' in the cotton instead of mine.* The sacks began to fill. She forgot about the overseer watching. She looked straight into the cotton bushes, stripping them bone clean.

She had once asked Liney how she learned to pick so fast.

"Pickin'. That's how I got strong. Pickin' faster each day than the one before. I put it in my mind to do it and my body just does it."

I gotta keep up with Liney. My legs are quick and so are my eyes. My ears are always listenin' even when Momma says they shouldn't. But my arms get tired so fast.

She remembered Liney's arms with their hard brown muscles pulling in the cotton. The older girl stood a half-foot taller so Phoebe always had to look up to her. Liney's slanted eyes sliced through her, noticing everything. Phoebe ripped out the cotton hard and fast, ignoring the sharp teeth of the boll against her fingers.

She glanced at Liney's children. She was glad her friend couldn't see them now. Bethy broke into tears whenever Phoebe looked at her and cried herself to sleep last night. She would not smile anymore. Phoebe had no answer but a sigh to Sarah's constant question. "Where's my momma?"

"Girl, do you hear?" Dianah's loud voice cut into Phoebe's thoughts. "Overseer's gone. Sit and rest for a spell. You pickin' a storm."

Phoebe thought of how far she had to go before she got as strong as Liney. She did not sit down with the older slaves.

"Emmett, it's your turn to sit. I'll keep watch."

"Sure do feel good to rest, Miss Phoebe." He stretched out on his back, singing snatches of a song, watching white wisps of clouds roll by high above his head.

When the sun comes back, and the first quail calls,
fol-low the drink-ing gourd.
For the old man is a-wait-ing for to car-ry you to free-dom,
if you fol-low the drink-ing gourd.

Phoebe liked the tune but couldn't follow the words. She knew the drinking gourd was a scooped-out squash shell slaves dipped into a bucket to drink from. *But some old man's gonna carry you to freedom? Just a song. A wish. Don't mean much.* She shrugged her shoulders and gathered cotton lightning speed.

For the next three weeks, Phoebe picked like Liney, each day weighing in one more cotton sack than the day before. Sometimes the Master and the overseer both stood by the edge of the field watching her, wrapped in stillness. When they left, Dianah and Emmett took turns resting. They sang out loud with the other workers, their words spilling over the rows. Sad and slow notes in the long mornings. Quick and snappy tunes to speed up the afternoons. Phoebe did not stop. All day long, her fingers spun to the beat of the music. Some lines rang in her mind over and over. *O hur-ry, an-gel! Hur-ry on down! With your wings and your snow-white gown!* The blisters on her fingers hardened and no longer bled. By dusk, hundreds of sacks overflowed with cotton.

They don't whip anyone now, Phoebe noticed. *The work is gettin' done. No time for daydreamin' when the sun's up. I gotta get finished on time. When the overseer's eyes are on me, he won't find anything to get mad at. He'll look right past without seein' me. He won't guess what I'm plannin' inside.*

Word came that Liney was getting better. She still couldn't chew or speak one word. Annie Mae fed her tea from bitter herbs that grew deep in the woods where no sun shone. One day, Phoebe heard Liney was sitting up and the next week, leaning on a cane.

Sounds just like Liney, thought Phoebe. *Mendin'. Gettin' stronger day by day. Just like a weed.*

Liney and her children would be safe on the Williams plantation now. Master Watson didn't want her anymore. No one wanted to buy a runaway. Phoebe had seen iron chains bind the feet of male slaves who tried to run away but never would again. She wished she could see Liney just once to tell her how much she missed her but she had promised her mother not to go. She could hardly wait for Liney to return to the fields.

"Why can't I check on her . . . just once?" Phoebe pleaded with her mother for the hundredth time.

"A child like you got no business messin' with a girl like Liney."

"I need a friend, Momma. Someone to talk to."

"That girl's a troublemaker. Stay away from her!"

"Liney had to run. Master sold her."

"She should have waited," her mother frowned. "Ran off like a rabbit."

"No time for her to plan," Phoebe explained. "One day she found out she was sold. That night she ran."

Her mother set one hand on each hip and leaned toward Phoebe.

"How did she find out she was sold? None of us house slaves knew 'til evenin' when Emmett told us."

Phoebe felt heat rise up her neck and spread across her face.

"You tell her, child?"

Phoebe nodded and hung her head down.

"You should get the switch for that!" Her mother's eyes darkened, her eyebrows meeting together like two thunder clouds. "I warned you about Liney. She's got a mark on her now. I forbid you to be her friend!"

"But Liney only . . ."

"Leave that girl be! Don't you ever go near her again!"

Phoebe's face stung as if her mother had slapped her. *Why does my momma hate Liney so? All the slaves sorrowed for Liney, alone with two babies and hurtin' bad. My momma's afraid of Liney.* Phoebe stared at her mother. For the first time, she saw panic in her mother's eyes, not anger. *My momma's so afraid that I will disappear on the underground railroad that she doesn't want me near anyone who's been on it, not even someone who can't talk about it! But I have to know! Who will tell me its secrets?* She flopped onto the floor. Beside the burlap sack lay Old Willie's cornhusk doll. She held it to her heart, its wings resting on her chest.

If you could take me there, where is it? She squeezed her eyes shut. She imagined a cotton dress, smooth and cloud-white. It brushed her skin softly. All at once, her feet lifted up like when Jake spun her around. This time, she heard fierce flapping as if a hundred crows passed by. Her arms ached. Water trickled below. She was searching for something. A sign. A single white star shone up ahead. She aimed her body toward it like an arrow to its target. She dreamed on.

Then one night, Phoebe slipped out the back window after her parents fell asleep. She stood a few minutes listening. Often a patrol of slavecatchers passed by to check that all slaves were inside their cabins. The patrol had the right to whip you hard if you were caught outside. But tonight, no one was around. She headed straight toward Old Willie's cabin just as if he'd been calling her.

She knew Old Willie didn't have much time left. Surely he could tell her something about the underground railroad. Outside his cabin, she could feel the stillness hang in the air.

No one's gonna give an ear to this but you. All I got is you right now to tell me what I want to know.

"Evenin', Willie. Do you remember me?"

The man in the bed was paper-thin. He did not move. His breath rattled in his chest like autumn wind through dry leaves.

"Come beside me, child. You be the one I'm learnin'?"

She paused. *Had Liney come here and Rachel before her?*

Willie lifted his hands trying to find hers, his face squeezed with pain. His eyes were wide open but the sight was gone out of them.

"It's Phoebe," she reminded him. "You taught me all kinds of things. How to make a proper fire. Hoot like an owl. You even talked about freedom. But you never told me how to get there."

"You wanna fly from here to freedom, girl?"

"Why, that's just what I've been doin' in my dreams!" Phoebe gasped. "There's a cold place I fly to. I'm light as a feather. Everything is white. And I'm so happy there, Willie."

She was close enough to see the change in his face, the smoothness, and his smile as he listened to her, as if the pain had gone away.

"That's how it comes to you, at first . . . in dreams. I'm flyin' myself now all the time. When I shut my eyes, it's there. Close by."

"But everybody calls me a dreamer like it's a bad thing." Phoebe hung her head down.

"Gotta dream, child," he whispered, "or you'll be stuck on this here plantation forever."

Willie lay flat with his eyes big and wide, looking up at the ceiling. "I remember something my daddy said," he whispered in a raspy voice. "If there's a way in, there's a way out. Slavecatchers brought us here. Not where we belong. All of us thinkin' and thinkin' just like my daddy there must be a way out. Well . . . there is."

"Where is it?" The words leaped out of Phoebe like flames.

"Ain't no easy place to get to."

"Why not?"

"Been a long road for me. Eighty long years and I'm just closin' in on it now. But for you young ones, it's miles and miles and just as hard." His voice faded.

"Who's the conductor, Willie? How can I get picked to go?" begged Phoebe. "Tell me quick so I can go ahead to this place I'm dreamin' about. My mind's so filled with dreamin' that my body feels as if it's in another place altogether."

Phoebe leaned her ear toward Willie's mouth to catch every single word but for long minutes all she heard was his breath.

"Been thinkin' on you, girl. You sound ready. In a mighty hurry, too. I'll tell you how to go."

"Why, Willie, are you the conductor?" Phoebe gasped. The old slave nodded at her. "Where is the road, then?"

"It's a railroad travelin' deep underground, girl."

"You mean beneath the earth somewhere?"

"It runs on the same ground we're standin' on but no one sees it. It's been runnin' ever since slaves first come here. Runs by a password. You don't get on unless you say, 'I'm lost.' If they answer, 'You are found,' you are on the underground."

Then Old Willie sang soft and slow to her.

The riv-er bank makes a ve-ry good road.
The dead trees will show you the way.
Fol-low the drink-ing gourd.

She remembered Emmett singing that song.

"How do you get on it?" she almost yelled.

Old Willie stopped to catch his breath. Phoebe heard loud wheezes whistling like a tea kettle in his chest.

"Song says to run to the river miles back of this plantation. The Conecun River, it's called. Keep your feet in that river the whole night. The moss growing on dead trees points north. So does the drinkin' gourd."

"Can you tell me where it leads?" Phoebe knelt beside Willie's bed. "I'm waitin' to go somewhere. I feel like something's bustin' out of me and gonna break loose if I don't get to it."

Willie nodded and reached out his hands.

"That's a freedom feelin', girl," he smiled. "You just wait 'til I rest up a bit. Come back in a few days. By and by, you'll have a pile of learnin'."

Old Willie shut his eyes. Gently Phoebe placed her warm hands on top of his and held them there until he fell asleep.

Now I'm gonna know something. She rushed back to her cabin. *See far past these rows of sea-island cotton. I'll make myself ready. My time will come. I just can't do nothin'. I don't even know if I'll stay here or be sold away. It's up to the Master. He's the king who owns me. But if I run, I'm the one to choose. Willie will guide me. He's the conductor I was searchin' for. Wherever I go will be better than here. I know the password to the underground. Now I just have to find where it runs.*

She could hardly sleep that night. Inside, she felt lit up with bright freedom light.

No Time for Dreamin'

August rains fell. Sweeping rain drove Phoebe out of the fields under the sheltering arms of the oak trees. Heavy rain churned the fields into mud. Swooping rain dyed the cotton dirt brown. Driving rain tapped on the tin roof of the cabin summer evenings. Then wind swept down clean from the north. The next day, the sky shone blue. The air was sharp and cool.

Phoebe skipped to the field. It was such a fine day, it felt just like the freedom Willie told her about. Free . . . dom! She stretched the word out in her mind like a drop of molasses. She imagined flying back and forth on the Williamses' swing, feet first, then her head touching the clouds. She and Liney could stroll through town in gingham dresses with white petticoats. But she couldn't go anywhere without the Master's permission. She had sneaked back and forth to the big house without anyone knowing, but she had never stepped off the plantation on her own. There would be a big whipping if she did.

What's the difference between us and folks at the big house? They're free and we're not. But we're the same inside. We all got a heart that beats and legs that run. Phoebe stroked her face, smooth and dark skinned. *Only our color's different. It's something they don't like. Something that makes them feel they can own us.*

She took a shortcut to the field and looked out across the long white rows. A feeling was building up in her chest, pushing to bust loose. She kicked a cotton plant so hard, all the bolls tumbled down to the ground.

This is the only place I know, workin' from sunup to sundown, livin' in Master's shadow, pickin' 'til my arms drop. I have no brother or sisters or even a friend to call my own. Gotta be a better place than here.

But that day everything changed.

At mid-morning, a woman trudged slowly across the field. The overseer galloped up to her in a cloud of dust and stopped. All the field workers, who had been watching, hung their heads down and picked.

"Kick you out of that bed finally, Liney," the overseer mocked. "If you try anything now, we'll be watchin'. At least we fixed it so you ain't gonna tell nobody."

Phoebe looked back up. Liney limped across the field. On her bare legs, the whipping scars gleamed. Bethy and Sarah stared at their mother numbly. No one spoke. No one moved. The overseer stood over them like a statue. Sweat trickled down Phoebe's back. She wanted to run to Liney and throw her arms around her, but she dared not even breathe. No one wanted her to be Liney's friend, not the Master or the overseer or even her own momma.

Afterward, the overseer rode off the field, but they could see him spying from the bushes. Liney picked wearily, as if it hurt her arms to lift them. The sacks filled slowly. Phoebe thought her friend had changed. Thinner. Leaner. Quieter. Her mouth was pinched as if she was squeezing her words inside. Liney had not been able to speak a word since she had been brought back. When she emptied her sack, her back was as stiff and bent as Emmett's.

At last the bushes rustled and the overseer rode off.

"Liney!" Dianah looked up. "We're pleased to have you back."

Liney kept her head down and picked as if she had not heard.

"Sit down for a spell and rest," offered Emmett. "I'll keep an eye out."

Liney raised her eyes with a look so forbidding that the sweat dripping down Phoebe's back cooled like a sheet of ice, making her shiver. Liney nodded her head toward the north where, half-hidden by trees, the Master's men watched them from horseback.

So many eyes watching them.

"They lookin' at us, sure enough," Dianah whispered. "Pick!"

When the men finally rode off, Phoebe immediately shot to Liney's side. Her hands gathered in cotton beside the older girl. Back and forth her fingers flew as if making music. Phoebe had practiced picking fast every day since Liney left. This was the day she had been waiting for.

Liney turned her head slowly toward Phoebe.

"Good!" her voice strained in one long syllable.

Everyone looked up at the sound of that one word. Every hand stopped picking. They all stared at Liney. Her voice was coming back. No one must know. Sarah grabbed her sister's hand and ran to Liney's side. Liney hugged her children for long minutes. But afterward, Sarah shrank back when Liney spoke to her, her voice odd and deep.

At first Liney's words were as slow in her mouth as molasses. She often lost her breath. When she said her first sentence, Phoebe danced around the cotton plants with her arms lifted up to the sky. Words, like deep and low notes from Liney's throat, were the music she longed to hear. *No matter what they did to Liney, they brought her back to me. I have lost everyone, but not her.*

Weeks passed. Questions hung unanswered in the hot field. *Where you been Liney? What was it like?* Phoebe did not dare ask.

"When you were gone," she wanted to tell Liney everything, "Master rode to the fields with the overseer to watch us."

"Checkin' that none of you got an idea to run. Seein' how you pick, too. You gatherin' cotton in a mighty speed since I left!"

Phoebe could hardly hear Liney. Her words were not clear yet.

"But they still spyin' on us, Liney, since you came back."

"Makin' sure I don't tell no one about the road. But

all the field slaves stay clear of me. That's how Master wants it."

The instant the overseer rode to the fields, Liney's back bent like an old woman's. The children stopped their games to watch. Phoebe and the others picked in a row by themselves as if they were too good to pick beside a runaway. But when he left, Liney straightened up and Phoebe flew to her side.

"You're just like a hawk," Phoebe admired her friend. "Seein' that overseer come a mile before he gets here."

"You pickin' fast. Growin' taller." Liney smiled. "Soon you'll feel him comin' too."

Phoebe smiled back at her and stood on tiptoe to show how tall she was growing. Liney laughed aloud, a low deep rumble that surprised them all. Her eyes were cinnamon warm again. Nothing, not even the whipping, could keep Liney down, Phoebe noticed. Nothing could make her hang her head for long.

Often Phoebe had a feeling that someone's eyes were upon her. She thought the overseer was spying but she could never find him. When she turned around, she caught Liney staring at her.

"You watchin' me, too, Liney."

Liney threw her head back and laughed. "Girls your age change from clouds to sun one moment to the next. Clingin' to your momma, then stirrin' up a storm to get what you want next."

Liney's eyes rested on hers, spicy warm. It was not the way her papa looked at her with eyes of sorrow or the crossness of her momma. She looked straight through her like she knew all of Phoebe's secrets.

"We picked side by side for one month, girl, but I never knew you. You're a deep-thinkin' girl, Phoebe."

Phoebe blushed. "You were kind to me in the fields. Even though you had big troubles of your own."

"Always did, girl!" sighed Liney. "Nowhere did I have someone to see me through. Emmett told me how you cared for my girls. You were my friend but I didn't know it."

"Your girls are still scared, Liney."

"I worry they're gonna live their whole lives in a shadow and never grow up strong." Liney shivered.

Phoebe looked at the two young girls. They sat still and did not play. She scanned the field in all directions. There was no movement in the bushes. No sign of the overseer. Yet a hush hung over the fields like the silence after a week-long storm.

The children's feet do not bounce down the rows of cotton anymore. Their voices do not ring out across the fields. No laughter anymore. No stories to pass the time. None of us dare stretch out and dream. Not a question from Sarah. Never a smile on Bethy's lips. I hoped they would be happy when their mother returned but they're still scared. That overseer sliced his knife through us all.

If you heal, Liney, Phoebe thought, *the rest of us will, too.*

Soon the overseer and Master didn't spy on Liney anymore. They had bigger problems. Slaves were disappearing. Sometimes one, then more, from the other plantations around the county. One night, a family of three disappeared from the slave cabins at Master

Watson's. Gone overnight. No one knew until the next morning when they didn't show up in the fields. The overseer rode with the slavecatchers and hounds after them. A week later, they returned with scowls on their faces but no slaves.

"That family must have found the road," hinted Phoebe, hoping Liney would tell her everything. "Maybe it goes underground. That's why they disappeared so fast on it."

From across the row she felt Liney's eyes bore a hole straight through her. "Freedom is a place, girl," Liney whispered between her thin lips.

Something leaped inside Phoebe. *The cold white place I'm dreamin' about! The colder it gets, the harder it is to fly. But nothin' will stop me from gettin' there.* She decided that now was the time to tell Liney about her dream, even the part about Liney flying beside her. She leaned across the cotton bush and grabbed hold of Liney's hand. But a shadow fell across the field blocking out the sunset. The overseer rode past for the check.

Dianah looked up. "No use talkin' about it now."

At home, Phoebe did not speak to her momma about Liney anymore. She kept her thoughts about Rachel for the night, too. There was no time to drift off in the fields anymore. *You went before me, Rachel. You never got caught or sent back like Liney. You just disappeared. It's as if you flew from here to there. If I follow your trail, I'll be safe, too. Tomorrow, I'll drop by Old Willie's. He'll tell me more.*

CHAPTER
NINE

Meeting in the Apple Orchard

That night, the hoot owls landed in the pines. Dusk dark. "Whoo! Whoo! Whoo! Whoo!" They screeched without stop until their calls echoed throughout the sleeping slave cabins. Phoebe lifted her head up from the floor, wondering.

"Death comin'," her father said quietly. "Somewhere nearby."

Next morning, Phoebe awoke to the murmur of voices outside. A group of slaves gathered around Old Willie's cabin, clutching their hats in their hands, heads bowed low.

"What are you millin' around here for? Get him in the ground and get to work!" the Master yelled.

He's gone! The thought flew to Phoebe's mind as if it traveled on the wings of a bird. She had not returned to Old Willie's cabin since that first visit. Patrols roamed the slave quarters each night. Too many running aways, slaves come and gone overnight from the nearby plantations. Now Willie was forever gone.

"But Master," a tall male slave begged, "Willie was like a father to us all. He needs a proper funeral first and then buryin'. That's our way."

"It's not *my* way!" the Master exploded. "Crops need pickin'. Bury him now! You got one hour. The rest of you get to work!"

The slaves marched slowly onto the fields. But Phoebe heard them one by one pass each other by and start to sing:

Steal a-way, steal a-way, steal a-way to Je-sus.
Steal a-way, steal a-way home.

By the end of the day, they all knew there was a meeting in the apple orchard. A meeting and a burying.

Two field workers kept watch that night behind the big house, ready to hoot if the Master stirred. The other slaves knelt at Willie's freshly dug grave at the back of the apple orchard. Mothers whose children had been sold away. Fathers whose weary shoulders sagged. Children who watched, wide-eyed. Toddlers who sucked their thumbs, clinging to their mommas' dresses. They prayed aloud the words they kept hidden in their hearts. The life of a slave they all knew. The sting of a fast whip. The scratch of the boll. An empty belly.

Only this peace and stillness of death they did not know.

Emmett led the service. "Willie found his freedom at last. Let's sing to lead him home."

Voices rose up like a flame lighting the dusk, singing a song Phoebe had not heard before.

Death song. Burying song. Joyful sound.

Toll de bell, An-gel, I just got o-vuh.
Toll de bell, An-gel, I just got o-vuh.
I just got o-vuh at last.

Phoebe closed her eyes. The words rippled through her body, raising goose bumps on her bare arms. She'd been dreaming about having wings and now Willie had his own wings to fly to freedom, the wings of an angel, like the cornhusk doll in her pocket. She pictured Willie lifting high above the cotton fields. He was floating like a feather, up and up.

If I just had two wings! she wished. *I'd fly to freedom too!*

She glanced across at Annie Mae. Her back was bent over like a weeping beech tree. But she lifted her white head up to the sky as if she saw Willie there, too. Tears ran down her face yet she was smiling sweetly.

Then it was Phoebe's turn to whisper goodbye to Old Willie. She said farewell to the child, too, who stopped by his cabin each morning as if he were her grandfather. The child she had been was gone, vanished in the cotton fields like smoke.

She did not stand beside her parents at the burying. She stood alone. Across from her, her father hung his head down, sorrows heavy on his shoulders. Behind her, she heard a rustle. Liney slipped a warm hand into hers. Phoebe shivered. Her touch felt familiar, just like Rachel's touch, as if her long-lost sister had come back to her. For the first time since her sister left, Phoebe felt her right beside her. Bethy and Sarah leaned on both sides of Liney and Phoebe, wrapped up in their own dreamplace. It felt just like family.

Phoebe felt her mother's eyes upon her, staring back and forth from her to Liney on the other side of Willie's grave. The deep pit opened up between them. Phoebe held fast to Liney's hand. Tears poured down her face without stop. Words welled up inside her, words that had no place to go before but spilled over now like spring rain. She wanted to scream them across the orchard. It was time for someone to hear. She didn't care if her mother knew.

I want to go to my dreamplace. I can't wait. I can't even wish anymore, 'cause the wishin' part, the dreamin' part, doesn't ever, ever stop and aches down deep. Who can I ask? Willie's gone. Rachel has vanished on the road without a trace. Liney almost made it but she won't talk. My momma forbids me to be her friend. I gotta know how to get out now. Don't let it disappear along with Old Willie. She squeezed Liney's hand. If only she knew how I felt!

Over and over, the words ached in her throat. She did not stamp her feet as she wished to do. She listened straight still. She waited for an answer. What she wanted was not here on the plantation. This was not home.

Home was someplace she had not been yet, just like freedom was a place — her dreamplace.

CHAPTER
TEN

Freedom Calling

One September night, Phoebe was almost asleep when an owl hooted outside her window. "Whoo! . . . Whoo! . . . Whoo!" She sat straight up. Again the hoot owl called. "Whoo! Whoo!" It was the call slaves waited for. She remembered Old Willie telling her she would know if it was an owl or a conductor. She rushed to the window. A dark shape hid behind two tall oaks.

Phoebe slipped out the back window in her bare feet. "Who's callin' me?"

A long brown arm reached out and pulled her behind the trees.

"I'm the one you're waitin' for." Liney's cinnamon eyes sparkled bright as gold. "I'll bring you to freedom. That's where you've been wantin' to go, isn't it?"

"But you didn't make it!" Phoebe protested. "I don't want to ever get caught. I'd just as soon be dead."

"I did it wrong, girl," Liney said, rocking her daughters,

one in each arm. "Broke out of here like a north wind. Twirled in circles. The slavecatchers trailed me with a torch. I'll never forget the gleam of their knife cuttin' me. I won't let that happen again. I met up with a conductor since."

"Who is he?"

"A slave who knew these woods like the back of his hand. He taught me that where stars come together in the shape of a drinkin' gourd, they point to the North Star, bigger and shinier than all the rest. Gotta follow it."

Phoebe remembered the song Emmett and Old Willie both sang. The directions were in front of her all the time, but she hadn't known it. She sang aloud some of the words.

When the sun comes back and the first quail calls,
fol-low the drink-ing gourd.
The riv-er bank makes a ve-ry good road.
The dead trees will show you the way.

"There's more I learned," whispered Liney. "Listen!"

The riv-er ends be-tween two hills.
There's a-noth-er riv-er on the o-ther side.
Fol-low the drink-ing gourd.

Liney rolled the words on her tongue as if they were poetry.

"That's where the road leads — in and out of woods and rivers to stop at safe stations in good folks' homes, all the way north. The first station is five hours upstream. Someone's gonna lead us from there."

Liney's eyes lit up the night. Phoebe wondered how Liney came through her beating stronger than ever. Liney stood so tall beside her, she seemed to hold her up, too.

"Why did you pick me, Liney? I'm just a kid."

"You're not a kid anymore. You're growin' so fast, you're almost as strong as me. I can trust you to move quick and think like lightning."

"But we can't leave now!" Phoebe suddenly understood the first words of the song. "The song says to go when the sun comes back and the first quail calls. That's spring!"

"We can't wait for no spring to come, girl."

Phoebe stood straight still, listening.

"Master Williams lost too much cotton in the heat. House slaves say in the auction next week, all the young girls will be sold. It happened to your brother and sisters. Dianah told me. I can't let it happen to you."

Phoebe gulped. Liney knew some of her secrets.

"You're leavin' with me and my children," Liney announced. "I can't do this trip alone. I need your help. But you gotta swear to tell no one."

"I promise, but . . . all of us are goin', Liney?" Phoebe looked wide-eyed at the girls asleep in Liney's arms.

"I shouldn't be bringin' 'em. But after that beatin', I swore my children wouldn't live like me." Liney hugged Bethy. "She's full of love and smiles inside that she can't let out. No Master's gonna get a chance to whip her."

"Isn't it risky, Liney?"

"They gonna slow us down and put us in danger for sure. But that's not what I'm worried about." Liney glanced down at her children. "It's them it's gonna be hard on. The conductor told me not to take 'em. Winter's hard on 'em, he said, but hunger's worse."

Phoebe lifted Bethy into her arms. She was a light bundle.

"We gotta take 'em, Liney. Maybe Williams will sell 'em. I know how to keep 'em alive — give 'em the first bite like my momma gave me."

Something shot through Phoebe like a lightning bolt. *My momma knows about the auction! House slaves hear everything first. She must be worried sick. She thinks it's safer to be sold like her other children. I have no choice but to run. I can't stay with my momma. Maybe, just maybe, she'll forgive me for runnin'.*

"Liney, was Old Willie your conductor?"

Liney looked at Phoebe. "Yes. When I came back all cut up, I felt like givin' up. But Annie Mae wouldn't let me. She kept talkin' to me about my babies, tellin' me to be strong. At night, she dragged me to her cabin and Willie whispered in my ear all he knew about the underground. He told me I'd make it next time."

"There was something about Old Willie. Always watchin' out for me," Phoebe smiled. "He couldn't go anywhere but he led me to believin' I could. He made sure I was smilin' every morning on my way to the fields, just like I was walkin' to my dreamplace."

"Where's your dreamplace?" Liney tilted her head to listen.

Phoebe hesitated. She wished she could tell Liney about her dream and how her new friend had flown beside her toward freedom. But there was no time now. Someone may be watching.

"Same place as yours . . . When are we leavin'?"

"Tomorrow night." Liney reached out and hugged Phoebe. "We'll be together, girl. Won't be so scared that way."

---— ◇ ———

CHAPTER
ELEVEN

Dream Star

In the field next day, Liney picked by herself as planned. Phoebe tried to concentrate on picking, but the memory of what happened last night set her mind on fire. Wads of cotton slipped from her hands into the dirt.

"Be careful, Phoebe!" whispered Liney from across the row. "Pick 'em up!"

Phoebe had nothing to pack for the trip except Old Willie's cornhusk doll, the one with wings. *The only belongings I really have are my parents and I can't take 'em with me*, she worried. *I can't even let 'em know what I'm plannin'. I promised Liney. My momma would stop me but what about my papa?*

Let us get away clean, she whispered to herself over and over again. *Let us get away clean.*

It must have been midnight when Liney called out from behind the oak tree. "Whoo! . . . Whoo! . . . Whoo!" Phoebe stood tall. She looked down at her parents asleep on the floor. Even in sleep, her mother frowned. Her father's face was soft. She knelt down beside them. From her pocket she pulled out the cornhusk doll and laid it gently between the two of them. *Forgive me for not stayin' with you. Don't worry none. I'll fly on Old Willie's words.*

She slipped out the back window where Liney waited with her two children, their eyes round as coins. Not a single star shone. *Better that way*, thought Phoebe. *We'll be hidden.*

She grabbed Bethy's hand. "You gonna run with me," she whispered, knowing soon she would carry the toddler on her back.

Bethy clung to her, hushed. But Sarah tugged her mother's arm.

"We gonna run now, Momma?"

They crept to the edge of the trees behind the cabins. They had just stepped into the thick woods when they heard voices. White men held torches high and led a pack of hunting hounds right past them. Liney stiffened. Slavecatchers! The two women clapped their hands over the children's mouths. Seconds passed like hours.

"He didn't come this way," declared a voice that Phoebe recognized as Master Williams'.

"Looks like that slave just ran clean away from Watson's place and didn't tell his mother Dianah nothin'. She's asleep inside," a slavecatcher announced. "Do you want to check all the cabins to make sure no one else went with him?"

"No!" yelled Master Watson. "We're wastin' time. Let's head back to my woods and check from there. He's already got a head start."

The men pressed on, holding a torn green plaid shirt in front of the hounds. Yelping wildly, the dogs yanked hard on their leashes and rushed ahead.

Jake! Phoebe had often seen Dianah's son wear that shirt at Saturday-night contests. She remembered his high jumps, his coffee-brown skin glistening in the moonlight as he flew through the air, his long legs spread out wide like some gazelle. And her holding her breath as she watched.

"Let's go!" hissed Liney in her ear. "We can't wait any longer."

"Maybe we shouldn't leave right now." Phoebe grabbed her friend's hand. "That's Jake's shirt. Those men will be out searching the woods for him tonight."

"Can't wait, girl! You gotta go with me or be sold!"

They did not speak again. Hand and hand into the dark night they ran. They headed toward the Conecun River that Old Willie said ran straight behind the Williams plantation. Liney's head twisted in all directions like an owl. Phoebe flew barefoot across the earth. She lifted Bethy onto her shoulders. Soon the child fell fast asleep leaning her head against Phoebe's neck. Phoebe did not feel the weight of her tiny body. She had no thoughts. Her mind was sharp and clear as the North Star.

Leaves rustled in the breeze like spoken words. A branch creaked on an old sycamore tree. Finally the river rushed nearby. They waded upstream. They could not run. They balanced carefully over slippery stones that cut into their bare feet. Sometimes tree branches hung over the water and hid them. Sometimes cornfields touched the riverbank. Often they had no cover and waded in wide-open spaces. They did not stop for an instant.

Sometime in the night, long after Phoebe lost track of the hours, they heard the faint barking of bloodhounds from the south. Liney stopped in her tracks, listening as she had in the field that day Phoebe told her she was sold. She listened as a tree does, still and tall, leaning into the wind. The barking loudened in their ears. Liney pointed upstream where thick willow branches waved like arms over the river. Lifting the branches, she motioned everyone to slip underneath. They squatted on cool, wet stones and let the water swallow their bodies until it covered their chins.

"Push on!" someone cried out. "Don't let them lose the scent!"

Hounds barked. Bushes crashed along the bank. Feet pounded the ground. Phoebe gasped so hard it hurt her to breathe. She leaned against Liney, her wet dress clinging to her body. Bethy and Sarah pressed against her, their heartbeats drumming hard against her chest. Phoebe's whole body froze like ice. Her heart seemed to pulse everywhere — deep in her belly, inside her ears, and even upon her lips. It beat so loud, she thought the slavecatchers could hear it.

Phoebe forced herself to think of something else. She imagined she was picking steadily, soft cotton brushing her fist. *Something to break the spell. Something to make time move. I'll mind my own business, look down at the ground. When the overseer's eyes are on me, he'll look right past without seein' me and leave me alone.*

Minutes passed. Phoebe imagined the hot sun on her back. She no longer heard her heartbeat in her ears. The hounds stopped by the water's edge near them, yelping wildly.

"He was here alright," a slavecatcher yelled. "Rested for a while and then went on. Here's where the tracks end. Must be farther upstream."

"Jake could be anywhere by now." Master Watson's voice drifted past. "He's my finest slave and I want him back. Let's hitch up the horses and round up more men. We'll see him better by day."

They led the hounds downstream. The barking faded.

Phoebe and Liney exhaled deeply and looked at one another. *Those hounds were so wild with Jake's track they couldn't smell what was right under their noses!*

Phoebe pushed herself up. There was one hour of darkness left. They waded upstream again. Just before dawn, when the sky was about to crack open, they noticed a meadow of blond wheat by the river's edge. A farmhouse nestled there. A single white star was painted on the red barn beside it.

Phoebe stopped by the water's edge, numb and cold, and stared ahead. It was the same star she had seen in her dreams. She remembered how it had suddenly appeared. She had been flying through darkness, the sound of water trickling beneath her, when she spied it. Without hesitation, she had flown straight toward it.

Liney pointed. "It's the first station! 'A star painted on a red barn by the river', Old Willie said."

She stepped out of the water and crouched low to the ground, Sarah riding flat on her back. Her sharp eyes sliced through the meadow in all directions.

Phoebe took a deep breath and lowered herself to the ground. She crept through the still yellow meadow while Bethy clung to her neck. She never took her eyes off the star. It shone like a promise.

Light edged over the horizon inch by inch. It grew brighter by the minute. It pulled her to a dreamplace where there was no cotton, no sun, and no slaves anymore.

PART TWO

---◇---

THE UNDERGROUND RAILROAD
FALL

Sometimes I feel like a motherless child,
a long ways from home.

C H A P T E R
T W E L V E

Star By The River

Phoebe stared straight ahead. She did not pause to check around her, as she had done all night. Dawn had arrived. They had to hurry to reach the station before the sun rose. She crawled behind Liney, wishing she could fly to the barn. Riding upon their backs, both children were quiet. When they were halfway across the field, Phoebe could see the white star on the barn distinctly. Five-pointed and bright, it pulled her like a magnet closer and closer.

Suddenly, Liney hissed a warning like a rattlesnake. Phoebe halted. Dried wheat stalks rustled ahead. Something was moving closer. Phoebe saw a white man headed through the wheat field straight toward them. His boots bent the tall stalks to the ground as he stepped nearer and nearer to them. She folded down into the wheat like a blade of grass.

"Who's there?" he called out.

He stood tall above them. There was no escaping him. "Just us slaves, sir." Liney looked up. "We are lost!"

A forever pause. Phoebe held her breath, ready to bolt away. Her hand reached out to yank Liney's arm when the man spoke again.

"You are found. Crawl behind me." Then he called in the direction of a farmhouse. "Whoo! . . . Whoo! . . . Whoo!"

A flutter of white appeared at the back window.

High above their heads, the sky brightened with light. They slid on their bellies over the dew-damp earth up to the door. A white woman motioned them inside through a kitchen into a pantry. The smell of fruit and mustiness hung in the air. The couple followed behind them, carrying a lit candle. Sarah snuggled against Liney, her big brown eyes watching the white woman's face.

"You're safe in here. I'm Eda and this is my husband, Amos."

Phoebe curtseyed as she was taught to do when white people spoke.

"Every couple of days, a slave knocks on our door." Amos shook his head. "About a month ago, a whole family arrived at our doorstep, and just last night, another runaway . . ."

Eda's face was lined with worry. "Friends, you'll hide with us for the day. Be still as statues. Tomorrow you run again."

In the deep shadow-dark of the pantry, Liney's head shot toward Phoebe's. Words sizzled in the space between them like lightning. *Where do we go from here?*

"You are on the underground now, the station by Brantley. A star by the river. From here on in, you must hide. Got a long journey north." Eda slipped out of the pantry.

"We'll ride together tomorrow morning," Amos instructed them. "Up to Montgomery to get my monthly supplies. I'll drop you near the next station. Folks won't pay any mind when a white man's wagon passes. But we may meet up with soldiers. Gotta be careful then."

"What do we do on the journey?" Phoebe whispered from a dark corner. Questions. Always questions. Old Willie had said that the underground was running many long years. She had to know where it led, find all the secrets the conductors knew.

"Be like a ghost from now on. Slavecatchers are all around us," warned Amos. "Step without a sound. Speak without a word. Follow one another like shadows. Folks might wonder if they saw a runaway, look again, and think it was just the wind."

Sarah shivered in her mother's arms.

"You know about the underground, sir," begged Liney. "What's the chance of us getting caught on it?"

"People get caught if they're scared. Hounds sure pick up that smell. You gotta keep strong and run fast. You'll be cold and hungry most of the time. Gotta be just one thing on your mind. Runnin'."

Phoebe remembered her parents' warnings about the underground and shuddered to hear them upon a white man's lips. She had not wanted to listen before. "Run like a rabbit with no food in your belly . . . Not for a family," echoed her father's words. *He was telling the truth!*

"How far do we run before we're safe?" she wondered.

They had heard they could stop once they reached Ohio, a free state. No slaves there. But there was another law: Fugitive Slave Law. They were not safe anywhere in this country.

"Gotta run all the way to Canada. If slavecatchers find you in any state, north or south," explained Amos, "they can drag you back for a reward. The law will punish you and folks who help you, too. Might take four months but you won't be free 'til you get there."

Four months! Phoebe realized with a jolt. *A long time. Rachel's been runnin' for three months. She could be comin' into Canada by now, if all went well.* She looked around the candlelit pantry with its deep shadows. *Did she hide like this, each night, with Samuel? Did folks like Eda help her too? Is she safe now?*

A double knock sounded on the pantry door. One hard knuckle followed by one light rap. Three times. Phoebe jumped.

Amos explained. "When you hear such a knock, it's the sign of a friend on the road. We cannot often speak with words so a signal will do."

His wife walked in with a breakfast tray and set it down next to them. She smiled at the girls and motioned them to take a bite. "After you eat, I'll lead you down to the cellar to sleep. We'll be about our business now." The couple left them alone.

Phoebe examined the tray with wide eyes. Fresh blackberries, soft and sweet. Fried white bacon.

Porridge. The hot food warmed her belly and made her yawn. She had not slept for the last two nights. She popped berries into the children's mouths. They swallowed them whole. Two knocks banged on the pantry door. One heavy. One light. Three times. Phoebe's head shot up.

"Come in," Liney's voice rang out.

Eda walked in with an armload of dry clothes.

"Hand me your wet dresses. I'll burn them. These clothes were donated by friends to help runaway slaves."

Phoebe held up the men's pants and shirt like a question.

"Slavecatchers will be out searchin' for four female slaves," Eda told them. "You will all look male. These colors will blend in with the woods."

Phoebe stepped into wide pants and drew the waist in snugly with a rope. She covered her shoulders with a brown flannel shirt and slipped into leather shoes. Meanwhile, Eda bundled the children into big woolen sweaters. As Liney changed beside her, Phoebe saw her swollen right leg and the whipping scars, gleaming red.

"Your leg ailin' you, Liney?"

"Started acting up in that river. Sure be nice if Annie Mae rubbed some healin' into it."

"If only I could wish it away like it never happened to you."

"Girl," Liney's voice was stern, "I'm gonna bear these scars my whole life. They'll remind me someday why I ran."

"You'll be walking across free ground by then. You won't mind such things any longer," Eda told them. She opened the pantry door wide. Bright sunshine flooded the kitchen. "We must hide you now. It's daylight and workmen will be at our door soon. Crawl behind me across the kitchen floor to the cellar door. Hurry!"

Phoebe and Liney slid out of the pantry. Bethy squatted inside the closet, squinting in the bright sunlight, hesitating. Sarah grabbed her hand but could not budge her. Liney had to pull the child out. Eda lifted a curtain in the corner of a hallway. Behind it was hidden a secret door. It opened onto a stairway leading down. The white woman handed them warm blankets and a lit candle. Ahead was pitch black.

"Light your way down and snuff it out. Try to sleep. You won't be alone —" Outside, wagon wheels screeched. "No more time to talk — go!" Eda shut the door behind them.

Phoebe lifted Bethy onto her back and headed down the stairs. Something scuffled below. She held the candle high, looking on all sides, watching dark shadows shift across the cellar room.

Ghost shapes.

A current of air touched her skin. Shivers whispered through her thin body.

"Who's there?" Phoebe held the candle high. "Show yourself!"

Something brushed against her feet. Someone appeared in the light of her candle. Dark, shiny eyes stared up at her from a handsome brown face.

Jake!

CHAPTER
THIRTEEN

Underground Dreams

Jake's shoulders loomed wide as the staircase as he stood below, looking up at Phoebe. Even in the candlelight, his brown skin glistened like chestnut. He was a good foot taller than she was and three years older. Master Watson was right. Jake was his finest slave.

"Phoebe, how did you get down here? And with a baby, too?" He lifted Bethy off Phoebe's back.

Phoebe gestured behind her. "Do you remember Liney and her babies?"

Jake smiled in recognition. "You just got to the Williamses', didn't you?"

Liney nodded as Phoebe held the candle closer to Jake's face. His eyes studied hers as he began to rock the child in his arms. Bethy had stayed awake half of the night, but now her eyes finally shut. *A trusting face. A field slave waitin' for us. The child must think she's back home.*

"When did you escape?" he asked.

"Midnight." Liney stepped down into the underground room. "We were right behind you. Seemed to be followin' your trail."

She peered through the shadows at Jake.

"How did you know I ran off, Liney?"

"Watson and his hounds passed by with your shirt lookin' for you. Dianah was sound asleep. That proved to them she didn't know where you went. No mother would be sleepin' if her son just escaped."

"Glad I didn't tell her," Jake sighed. "She never wanted to hear about the underground. Didn't see how slaves could run on it. Well, we have disappeared from the earth this morning as if we walked clear off it."

"When we were in the fields, Dianah always hushed me," Liney told him. "'Too much talkin',' she said. Didn't want no one to fuss about freedom."

"There's a reason why she's edgy about freedom. 'Cause of my daddy." Jake's face darkened like thunder clouds. "Once the overseer whipped her 'cause she dragged her feet after workin' twelve hours straight. My daddy snapped. He hit that overseer hard. They whipped my daddy, strung him up, and hung him dead. Ma and me, we had to watch. I ain't never forgot how my daddy died — fightin'."

"With me, it was runnin'," confessed Liney. "That's all I thought about since I was ten. Freedom grew in my mind like a wild weed. Nothin' could stop it. Not even Master Williams."

"Williams!" Jake scowled. "Used to watch me every

second to catch me up. Old Willie said, 'You got too much fire, boy. Master's gonna see it.' Then, when I got sold to Watson, I couldn't be a slave no more."

"You got plans to head a certain way?" Liney questioned him.

Jake looked back and forth from Liney to Phoebe. "Just gonna run where Old Willie said to go. Fast as I can."

All this while, Phoebe stood spellbound on the stairs, studying the fire in Jake's eyes, wild and bright, like Old Willie said. Yet something about Jake was warm and rich as honey, too.

"Phoebe, what are you doin' here, child?" Jake turned toward her. "Everybody talks about freedom but nobody runs."

The word "child" swept through Phoebe like cold wind. *I am no longer a child. I am old enough to have babies. Old enough to run.*

Phoebe folded her arms across her chest. Tears smarted in her eyes. Her thoughts jammed up inside and she could not speak.

"Phoebe knew runnin's dangerous. And still she wanted to come," Liney said.

Jake watched Phoebe step down the stairs and stand by Liney's side. "I been wantin' to run for a while," she told him. "Liney knew it was the right time to go."

"But what made you ready, Phoebe? You always seemed so peaceful like, workin' in the fields across from me, pickin' your fill."

Jake's bright smile reached down inside Phoebe like

a ray of Alabama sunshine in the damp underground tunnel. She could tell them both now. "Dreams kept comin' to me. I didn't know what they meant 'til Willie died. He had peace. I wanted it too. In my dreams, I just fly there. It's that quick. Pass through water and cold to a great, white dreamplace."

"Your words sound just like music, Phoebe," admired Jake. "It's what we're all lookin' for — freedom. A chance to live our own dreams, not someone else's."

Sarah leaned against Phoebe and took the candle out of her hands. She searched along the tunnel on tiptoe, holding the candle high, checking each dark corner with Liney at her side.

"No ghosts here, Momma," she whispered. "That man said we gotta act like ghosts from now on. What did he mean?"

"We gotta hold our breath 'til we're free," answered Liney.

"Wonder what it's like on free ground?" Phoebe recalled her father's words. "I hear we can own land. Keep our families together."

"I dream we're never gonna be hungry there or whipped anymore." Jake looked down at Bethy asleep in his arms. "No more runnin'. No scared looks on these children's faces. We're all gonna be safe there."

Liney shook her head at them both and frowned. "I sure don't let myself dream about it. Believe it when I feel it beneath my feet. Not a minute before."

"I dream about a better life all the time," said Phoebe. "Dreamin' runs through my family. My grandpa dreamed of Canada. And my sister Rachel escaped three months ago."

"You never told me that!" Liney's mouth fell open.

"I didn't know where she was. The night you ran, my parents told me the truth — that she chose to run, rather than be used by the Master. I been waitin' to follow her ever since."

"She's well on her way now," Jake said. "Maybe we'll meet up with her in Canada."

A pause. Liney faced Jake straight. "You plan on joining up with us, Jake?"

Phoebe's heart skipped a beat as Liney asked the question she dared not. Ripples of emotion passed over Jake's face, so near to hers that Phoebe felt she could reach out her hand and touch him.

"I had planned on runnin' alone. But you women are travelin' with children," Jake shared his thoughts. "No one knows the woods like I do. We'll be safer together," he decided.

"You could help us, Jake." Liney told him.

"Maybe so. But if trouble comes, we may have to separate. I'll teach you all I know first so you can go on by yourselves."

Phoebe heard Jake say yes. But she heard something else, too. *Women.* She repeated it over and over in her mind like a chant. *I am a woman to him now, someone different, not what I was on the plantation. A cotton picker. A dreamer. Just a child. He's comin' with us.*

They covered the children with blankets. Bethy had already fallen asleep in Jake's arms. And now Sarah, once placed beneath the warmth beside her sister, closed her eyes too. Their bodies lay limp, their faces soft and trusting in the quiet. Then there was calmness, the darkness of this cellar room filled with friends. They had escaped from the world into an underground room tunneled out of the earth. They stood still until the candlelight flickered and dimmed on its short wick. They remembered what they had been told.

Become like ghosts tomorrow, Amos warned us. And Eda told us to snuff the candle out. Sleep. Tomorrow, you run . . . We have to rest now. We may not have this time again. Perhaps tomorrow, our hearts will pound with each new step. Our bellies will be empty. The dark night will deepen around us. Tomorrow, the fear again. But for now, we are safe here.

Liney lifted the blanket and slipped beneath it with her children. Phoebe curled up beside them. Jake lay down at their heads and blew the candle out. His face was the last thing Phoebe saw before darkness fell like a cloak of black velvet.

CHAPTER
FOURTEEN

The Road to Montgomery

In sleep, Phoebe stretched her arms out wide. One arm flung across Liney and the other across Jake. In her dreams, she was flying across a dark sky, reaching out both her wings. All night long, she listened to loud flapping, wondering if a whole flock of crows had joined up with her. It pumped a steady rhythm in her ears.

Long before dawn, Phoebe awoke, wide-eyed, on the cold earth floor. *Why, it's all of us flyin' together! Two friends beside me, pumpin' their wings strong. Tiny wings below me, flutterin' to keep up, the wings of children. All five of us headed to Canada.* She propped herself up on her elbows, thinking about the trip ahead and how she would run to the dim white place. Nearby, Bethy slept deeply, her body hot as a little stove. Phoebe smoothed the child's cornrows with her fingers, tying up the loose ends in the darkness, wondering how far away Canada was.

Then the double knock. Three times.

"Wake up!" whispered Eda from the stairway. "Amos is hitching the wagon."

Jake jumped to his feet. Bethy whimpered until Phoebe rocked her. Liney folded a blanket around Sarah. All eyes followed a streak of white light up to the door. They shifted like shadows toward it and inched upstairs.

"Put these caps on, girls." Eda tucked Phoebe's thick braids under her cap. "Here's blankets and breakfast. Not one word in that wagon. Promise me now. Send Amos back to me safe."

As they passed through the back door, Phoebe caught a glimpse of herself in the hallway mirror. She did not recognize her own face. Thin. Long. Dark eyed. Half-hidden beneath a dark wool cap with a wide brim. Bulky clothes covering her shape. She was neither female nor field slave any longer. She had become a young black boy.

Outside, a wagon was hitched to an old mare. Amos lifted a flap at the back of the wagon and motioned them inside.

"Lie down on top of the hay. If I slow down, listen. If I stop, don't even breathe. Checkpoints ahead. If there's trouble, I'll knock a double knock." Amos tapped a board behind the driver's seat. "Keep those babies still, whatever you do!"

Amos jerked the horse's reins, "Heigh ho!" and rode off.

The wagon tilted up and down over the ruts in the road. They shared a breakfast of blackberry muffins and passed a tin of water from hand to hand. No one spoke.

Once Sarah opened her mouth to ask a question but Liney hushed her with a stern look. At last, they settled in together, Jake's long legs touching Phoebe's and the weight of the children on top anchoring everyone down.

Now they could drift, shut their eyes, and be rocked into rest as if suspended between the old world and the new. Each lift of the mare's feet carried them farther away from the cotton fields of the South onto the underground road.

Phoebe felt a melting down, a deep, delicious melting down as if her life spun around and around. In that spinning, she saw the South. Fields of cotton spread out flat beneath the sky. Old Willie waving from beneath the apple trees. Her parents on the back porch, talking. Emmett singing, deep and low. It was close by yet far away, some miles behind her. She could not turn back.

Gone.

Hours later, the carriage slowed down in bright sunshine. The wagon crept slowly forward as if not certain where it was going. A double knock rapped hard against their heads. Everyone sat up straight still.

"Whoa!" a man yelled. "Stop for check!"

"Alright, soldier." The wagon shuddered to a stop.

Inside, bodies shifted on the straw.

"Where are you headed?" a man asked beside the side flaps.

"Up to Montgomery for my month's supplies. Tired of this rocky road you got here."

"Seen anyone?"

"Nope. Just me and my horse."

"No darkies?"

"Nope."

"We got news of a group of five escaped. Two women, two children, and a young man. Maybe they're runnin' together. There's a fat reward out for the male. Seen signs of anyone?"

"No, soldier. It's been right quiet."

A long pause. The mare kicked its hind legs. Sarah leaned forward to listen. Then Phoebe heard the question she had prayed would not come.

"What you got inside?"

Liney's eyes shot toward Jake's.

"Fresh meat. Blankets. Going to trade 'em for flour and sugar."

"Your horse looks mighty tired to be carrying such a light load."

"This mare's old. Plumb tired out, is all."

"Let's check." The soldier's footsteps halted by the wagon.

Quicker than a thought, the spear of a gun poked through the flaps. Its sharp point cut into Jake's thigh. He flinched, squeezing his lips together to hold back a scream. In the next instant, the spear slipped out again. Liney's hands, that once flew over cotton, reached out and lightly wiped the blade clean.

"Nothin's livin' in there," the soldier laughed. "Move on. Be on the lookout for slaves. Not safe to be out."

"Heigh ho!" The wagon jerked unevenly as Amos drove on.

Jake collapsed back onto the straw. Blood poured from

his thigh. He pressed his hand hard on top of his leg to stop the bleeding. Phoebe wanted to reach out and touch him but dared not move.

"Are you alright?" Amos slowed the wagon.

"Jake's hurt!" Liney did not whisper this time.

The wagon halted. Light streamed in through the back flap showing a long red cut sliced through Jake's flesh. Amos handed them a jug of water with clean white handkerchiefs.

"Clean it up good. Don't leave one trace of blood in this wagon."

Jake winced as Liney cleaned his wound with the wet cloth. Afterward, Amos buried the bloodstained handkerchiefs in the woods. The wagon rolled on.

All this time, Sarah had watched Jake with wide eyes. Suddenly she could not hold back her tears any longer, tears that had frozen inside since she was carried away from the plantation two nights ago.

"I wanna go back home, Momma!" she cried. "Jake's gonna die!"

Bethy's bottom lip trembled a moment, then she, too, screamed out loud. Phoebe hugged her but could not hush her cries.

Amos slammed a warning knock against their heads.

"Jake's gonna be fine." Liney's jaw clenched. "We're goin' off to find a new home, that's all. Shush!"

"Where are we goin'? I don't like it," Sarah sobbed.

"To freedom, child," her mother coaxed. "There'll be a soft bed for you there with pillows and a feather cover."

Sarah kicked her feet up and down in the straw and

screeched wildly. This time, Amos pounded his fist against the board loudly.

"I'm hurtin' and you're the one who's carryin' on!" scolded Jake. He lay back in the straw. Sarah and Bethy crawled over to him and cautiously looked down. Jake opened his arms wide and winked. They both giggled and piled on top of him as if he were a warm bed. Phoebe smiled. Before this trip, they never even knew Jake but now they curled up on him as if he were their father.

Liney noticed Phoebe watching her children with Jake.

"They had a fine daddy once. A strong man. Long gone."

"Who was he?" Ever since she met Liney, Phoebe had wanted to know.

"Gone. I promised not to speak his name again."

Liney turned away, back into silence. Phoebe wondered who he was and where he went and why Liney let him go.

The young girls drifted off to sleep. Phoebe's mind whitened as if all thoughts left her. *This is what I've been dreamin' of! The cold white land stretchin' out ahead of me.* Around midnight, when owls hooted from the deep woods, the wagon halted. The runaways crawled out.

"This is your stop. We're past Montgomery," announced Amos. "Study this map. It'll lead you to the next station, through these woods to the mapmaker's, at Elmore."

He held up an oil lamp over a thin piece of paper. On it was sketched a rough drawing of the woods, with arrows pointing to the mapmaker's station. It had no words, only pictures. Slaves could not read. It was against the law to teach them. On top of the map was the North Star leading the way. On the bottom stretched the cotton fields of the South. On the right side was sunrise: East. On the left, sunset: West.

"Memorize this. Make your own minds like a map to see you clear to the North. Then get rid of this paper. Leave no trace behind!"

Not a single star shone. A strong wind blew from the north. A storm was coming. Jake's hand shot out to shake Amos's.

"Thank you, friend, for showin' us the underground."

"It's the mapmaker's job to do that. Farewell!"

They scattered into the woods like leaves into the north wind. Bethy pressed flat against Phoebe's body, wrapping her arms around her neck. Phoebe's feet skimmed over the earth. Her body felt loose and free, as light as if she had wings. She was flying fast just like in her dreams.

This is what I know how to do, she thought. *This is what I was made for. Runnin' hard.*

When they slipped deep in the woods, Jake ripped the map into a thousand pieces. The paper flew in little white clouds back to the South, to the land of sun and slaves and row after row of sea-island cotton. They turned their backs to it and headed straight into the wind.

The cool north wind.

CHAPTER
FIFTEEN

The Mapmaker

Phoebe guessed it was near dawn by now. The sky was touched with a hint of gray. Raindrops sifted slowly down through the trees. *The mapmaker's station must be near*, Phoebe thought wearily. *Maybe we passed it by.* She stopped short, forcing Jake and Liney both to halt. A bat fluttered by their heads. A tree limb creaked like an old person's bones.

Then there was a snap of a twig underfoot. Right behind them.

Jake dropped Phoebe's hand and limped away with Sarah upon his shoulders. Phoebe remembered him warning them that they might have to separate if they ran into trouble. No one could track them all down that way. *Too sudden! Too soon!* Phoebe and Liney headed across the forest in the opposite direction. Liney squeezed Phoebe's hand as they ran fast side by side, hearts pounding as one, weaving a crooked path in and out of the trees. A tree branch scratched Bethy's face as she sat propped high on Phoebe's back. The child awoke screaming, not knowing where she was. Phoebe yanked Bethy down and pressed her to her chest to hush her.

Click! A gun loaded. A bullet slid into a chamber.

Dead ahead.

"Stop!" someone ordered. "Who's trespassin' in my woods?"

They could see the man's wrinkled white face and his clothes, sewn from deerskin. Then the gun pointed at their heads.

"Here I'm huntin' possum in my own woods and I find two slave boys instead. Cartin' a baby, too. What are you doin' here?" he demanded.

"We are on our way home, sir. Sorry if we trespassed."

"Where are you goin'?"

Liney hesitated a second. "We are lost, sir."

The password! The man didn't say a word in response. Phoebe sucked in her breath. In her arms, Bethy stiffened.

"Who sent you?" He shot out the question like a bullet.

"We are lost, sir," Liney tried again.

"You are found." He unloaded his rifle. "Was it Amos who sent you?"

"Yes, sir. To look for the mapmaker."

"I'm the mapmaker." He turned his head and spat. "Can't trust nobody nowadays. Black folks sometimes turn out to be spies, too. Fightin' against their own side. You be on the lookout for 'em, hear?"

Liney nodded.

"Is this all of you?"

"There's two more," a deep voice shouted behind them.

The mapmaker spun around with his gun aimed straight.

"Don't shoot!" yelled Jake. "I'm another lost slave."

"Three young boys! Runnin' with babies, too. You're brave, all of you. Follow me. I gotta hide you before dawn."

He lived in a cabin deep in the woods. No road led to it and no path. Tiny windows looked out from each side of its walls. Inside, it was snug and dry as a drum.

"Months go by without my seein' a soul. But things are changin' now," said the mapmaker. "War's on. Soldiers travelin' north and south. Slaves slippin' through my woods. If I put my ear to the ground, I hear it shake with all the runnin'."

Jake told the mapmaker about the checkpoint. He pointed to his ripped pant leg. Through it, Phoebe could see dried blood. The mapmaker handed him a hot, wet cloth to press over the wound. They had dared not stop to clean it during the night.

"That was the Confederate Army after you. Got orders to capture runaway slaves. Kill you if you run. Yankees comin' through, too. Slaves hidin'. My job is to sit in the middle, leadin' slaves north."

"Folks like you," said Jake, "risk your lives for us."

"Son, I'm a man who lives his own way. Nobody tells me what to do. That's how I believe everyone should live."

Phoebe leaned sleepily against Liney as the mapmaker spoke. "Look at me runnin' my mouth and forgettin' my hospitality. We'll talk later. I'll fry us up some breakfast first."

The mapmaker busied himself at the woodstove. An odor of cooking grease filled the room. Sarah and Bethy chased one another in circles around and around the stove, just as they once played in the fields. The cabin echoed with giggles.

"Those little ones need to have some fun. Runnin's serious business. You be the mother?" he asked Liney.

She nodded and smiled at her children running free.

"I thought you all was boys but now I see there's only one." The mapmaker grinned a toothless grin. Everyone looked at Jake and laughed. The sound of laughter was new to them and shook their bodies with light. It seemed a long time since Phoebe had heard such merriment.

The smell of hot bacon grease and fried onions drifted to Phoebe's nose like a call home to her momma's cooking. Her stomach flipped over. White folk's food. She remembered stolen bites in the Master's kitchen, hot and sweet, and how her mother sneaked treats into her mouth with her fingers. The mapmaker flipped hushpuppies in an iron skillet, then tossed her a steaming one.

"Catch!" he called out.

Phoebe looked up, startled. The food burned her fingers and slid down her throat salty hot, just like it was supposed to.

"Hope some things in the South don't change," he laughed.

At last they sat down over a pot of mustard greens and onions. It looked like Jake would never stop eating but he finally wiped the pot clean with the last hushpuppy. The mapmaker sat back and lit his pipe. After a few puffs, he placed a tray on the table and poured fine white sand into it.

"This is where I draw my maps." He smoothed the sand out with his palm. "When you leave, you'll recite it all back to me. Then I'll wipe this one flat. No one's gonna guess where you've gone."

They gathered around the warm stove. The girls stretched out on their mother's lap. Their bellies were full and their legs hummed from running around the cabin. Soon they were yawning.

The mapmaker sunk his finger into the sand and began to trace a trail. "Follow the rivers as much as you can. Ride the Coosa River 'til it ends in a big lake. Weiss Lake. Come a swamp then, likely to get lost in it. Time stands still there and hides you. Head northeast into the Smoky Mountains. A good hidin' place, far from anyone. Stay low down, on the ridge. When the mountains lead east, head down. Be on the lookout for many rivers."

"Old Willie told me that many rivers lead to the Ohio River," Jake recalled.

The mapmaker nodded. "When you're out of the Smokys, follow the rivers west until you reach a wide river. The Kentucky River. You'll know you're on it if you pass by a small mountain. If you're lucky, boatmen will ferry you across it to the Ohio River. Watch for lanterns flashin'. Boatmen's signal."

"Something else I remember Old Willie sayin'," Liney added. "Told me Ohio was a free state. Quakers livin' there. Stations dottin' it up and down."

"There'll be many friends in Ohio to shelter you. Your trip will be halfway over by then," instructed the mapmaker. "Head north to a port town. Sandusky. Sail across the lake to Canada. Once you're over the border, you're free. Never be a slave again."

The young slaves looked at one another with wide eyes. They hadn't thought much about what they would find in the North, just about getting there. *Never be a slave again.* Canada was a dreamplace. Cold. Shadowy. Far away.

"Never let yourself be seen. One little thing can give you away," the mapmaker warned. "Travel only at night and never on a full moon. Hide in fields. Sleep in barns but run out before dawn. Once you're on the Ohio River, you'll need to build a raft to sail on it. Find logs in those barns to build it. You'll switch to another river, the Scioto. Follow it straight up."

"It's just like the song says!" Phoebe exclaimed. "The riv-er bank makes a ve-ry good road. There's a-noth-er riv-er on the oth-er side."

"That's a song most slaves sing without even knowin' it's a map. Sing it right under the Master's nose, too." The mapmaker grinned.

The Ohio River. Phoebe remembered all she'd heard about it. Swift and wide, some said it was, with flat farmland on all sides. It gleamed in her mind like promised land.

It's a long way to go. There'll be no comin' back, thought Phoebe. She shut her eyes and curled up by the wood stove. She saw herself walking and walking for days. Days turning into months. On all sides of her, the mountains rising up to hide her. The Ohio River rushing past. The cold land stretching out at the end of the journey. *No comin' back. No comin' back.* The rhythm of the words pounded in her ears like running feet. She held her breath, listening to it. She was hoping to hear Rachel's footsteps speeding north, too, but the mapmaker's voice loudened instead. "You'll reach Canada by Christmas, if all goes well," she heard him tell her friends. "Best to reach it before deep winter. Before the snow. Before the waters freeze."

Phoebe had never seen snow before but now imagined its cold whiteness falling down. To her, it felt like freedom. *Let us pass over to Freedom Land. If all goes well.* She soon fell asleep on the cabin floor.

She never knew that when everyone fell asleep that morning and the mapmaker returned to his hunting, Jake lay upon the floor beside her and followed the play of firelight over her sleeping face. He watched the sharp hills of her cheekbones, the smooth brown skin of her face, and the way her braids loosened, her shiny black hair falling down her back. He thought he saw dreams light up her face and he wondered what they were.

Makin' Your Mind Like a Map

"Are you awake?"

Phoebe watched Liney's eyes flicker open. Phoebe was already sitting up, wrapped in blankets, eyes shining bright as sunshine as she looked around the mapmaker's cabin. She felt stove-warmed and safe. In her parent's cabin, she could not say what she was thinking aloud. Shush! her mother would warn. But she could tell Liney everything now.

"I dreamt a new dream."

"Was it your dreamplace?" Liney stretched herself awake.

Phoebe squeezed her eyes shut again, trying to remember. The dream had gleamed brightly inside her mind when she first awoke, but now it was fading.

"Gray skies. A cold white light . . . Tiny specks fallin' without stop. Maybe it's snow. Twirlin' harder and harder in all directions."

Liney propped herself up and listened intently to Phoebe. In the far corner of the cabin, Sarah and Bethy sprawled on a bearskin.

"Four people," whispered Phoebe. "Walkin' on and on. Covered with snow. Lookin' up at the sky. They lift up and disappear."

Phoebe's words traveled through them both with a shiver. *Four people! What does that mean? There are five of us.*

"Snow's ahead," Liney simply said. "Nearer we get to Canada, the more chance of it. Be no dream once we get there. Be cold and hungry by then."

"Ever since that day you talked about the underground railroad, these dreams of travelin' started comin' to me," Phoebe told Liney for the first time.

"I never dreamed about it," said Liney. "All I wanted, soon as I was sold to Williams, was to find out about the road."

Jake stretched himself awake. "Wish it was easy to follow, like sleepin' and dreamin' is."

"Did you dream, too, Jake?" asked Phoebe.

"Just sleep hard is all. It's the only time I can forget I'm a slave. I want freedom. I'll fight anyone who stops me from reachin' it."

"How you gonna fight?" scolded Liney. "If anyone sees you, they'll kill you first. Ask questions later, like the mapmaker said."

"I heard what the mapmaker said. War's on. Sides are linin' up. Maybe that's what I gotta do."

The mapmaker appeared in the open doorway holding a skinned raccoon.

"Best you leave fightin' to the army, son. Get yourself safe to Canada instead. I'll cook you all a right good meal before you go."

"You gonna stuff us so much," joked Jake, "we won't be able to run."

"Better eat your fill, son. May be your last hot meal for a long while."

Liney gathered her children around the table. Bethy watched quietly as everyone ate but she wouldn't taste one bite.

"If you don't eat it up, I'm gonna wolf it down!" Jake pretended to scoop up bites of her steaming stew with his empty spoon.

"What's the matter, child?" Liney asked her.

"It smells!" whined Bethy. "Got stuff floatin' in it."

The mapmaker peered into her bowl and slapped his leg. "That's meat!" he laughed. "You ever tasted it?"

"She hardly ever ate it," said Liney. "Doesn't remember it."

"You want to run to freedom, girl?" the mapmaker asked.

Bethy looked at her mother.

"Freedom's the place we're headed," Liney reminded her.

Bethy nodded at the mapmaker.

"Then wolf that stew down like Jake says! Gonna make you strong. Runnin' strong."

Bethy screwed her lips up and looked down at the stew. Jake nudged her and pointed to Sarah's clean bowl. Slowly Bethy dipped her spoon and ate.

After they finished supper, the mapmaker turned to them one by one and asked them questions. Remembering questions.

"There are three of you leadin', but you must be as one," he reminded them. "What one forgets, another will remember."

Phoebe guessed what the mapmaker did not say. *And if we separate*, she thought, *we will share the same memory. Only four of us ran in my dream. One of us was missin'. Each of us will have a map to Canada printed in our minds. Maybe we will find the way back to one another, maybe not. At least we can go ahead.*

"How do you follow the Coosa River?" asked the mapmaker.

Jake answered, "Head north until the lake ends. Cut through a swamp."

"How many days is the trip through the Smoky Mountains?"

Phoebe's turn. "Fourteen days. No stoppin'."

"What are the river signals?"

Sarah's turn. "Blue and yellow lantern lights blinkin'."

"What is the name of the guide in Sandusky?"

Liney's turn. "Reynolds."

To each question, they answered right and true. The mapmaker leaned back with a wide grin.

"Mountains and rivers, children, hug 'em tight. Harder to trace your trail through 'em. Slavecatchers will be blockin' all roads to the North. You gotta outsmart 'em. Run every which way around 'em."

He guided them that night to the Coosa River before

saying farewell. Then they were alone except for a million stars above their heads.

"Let's study 'em to make sure we're going straight," whispered Jake.

Phoebe nestled on the ground at the edge of the river between her two friends with the children lying warm in her arms. She had never lain awake under stars before with no roof between her and the sky. She looked up — so many stars, such a wide sky. There was no black space left, just light. The drinking gourd pointed to the North Star, the biggest and brightest of all the stars. Phoebe marveled at how clear it all was.

A map was there all along to lead me, only I didn't see it. This star map just lay across the sky, pointin' to another world. The answer is lyin' just above our heads.

They stepped into the river without a word. Phoebe kept staring up at the sky, up and up, with a wondering smile. *Freedom sky.* The night cloaked them in blackness. Once again, they were alone, wading in night waters. They felt the muddy river bottom beneath their feet. Somehow it felt like home.

CHAPTER
SEVENTEEN

Poor Boy

They traveled at night, by a sliver of a quarter moon that grew round in the sky like a coin. Sometimes owl hoots broke the spell of the night. Sometimes rabbits screeched. Always, muddy water lapped against their legs.

Silence. Signals. Little sleep. Children were rocked from hand to hand. Looks passed back and forth between them instead of words. They had memory, too. Phoebe reviewed the mapmaker's directions over and over, picturing a map in her mind.

Sometime in the third week as they searched for a safe spot to rest for the day, they heard someone singing an old folksong slaves in the South knew by heart.

Some-times I'm up.
Some-times I'm down.
No-bo-dy knows the trou-bles I see.

They stood knee deep in the waters, listening. *Probably*, thought Phoebe, *it's the voice of an old slave on his way to the fields.* She imagined his work-worn face. Jake inched forward, stepping out of the river. The two women tiptoed behind him.

An old black man in tattered trousers sat on the riverbank. He leaned toward them. "Is there five of you runnin'?"

"Yes." Phoebe smiled to see that it was, indeed, an old slave sitting there. "Who are you travelin' with?"

"Myself." He eyed Jake's sack. "Walked all the way from Florida and got plumb tired and hungry, too."

"We're just about ready to stop. Maybe you'd like to share our food," offered Liney. "Been a long time since we met a friend."

"Sit right down and get yourself dry for a spell," the old man readily answered.

They shared the last of their supplies. Crumbs of cornpone. Strips of possum meat. Dried berries. The mapmaker had loaded up their backpack and they had eaten only a handful each night but after this meal, it would all be gone. Afterward, Liney and the girls curled up and fell fast asleep.

"Which way should I go to find a safe station, boy? Do I keep to the river or head over land?"

Jake shot a look at Phoebe, then hinted, "Depends how lost you are."

"Oh, I've been lost since I left Florida." There was no change in the old man's face. "Tell me which way's safe for slaves to go."

"Near dawn now. Time we settled in and were quiet. Let's go to sleep and tonight we'll tell you all we know." Phoebe thought she heard Jake's voice tighten like a fist.

"But, son, we could waste time that way. I'm an old man. Takes me a long time to learn." He limped over to a cottonwood tree and sat down.

"We've walked a long way and need to rest," insisted Jake.

"I heard tell of a slave hurt near Montgomery." The old man stared straight at Jake's torn pant leg. "Hounds dug up handkerchiefs with fresh blood on 'em. Been followin' his trail ever since."

"No more questions, old man," Jake ordered. "Go to sleep!"

Silence sparked in the air like lightning before hard rain. Phoebe closed her eyes and pretended to sleep but her mind was all lit up. She lay wide awake on the cold ground. *That old man knows too much. "Be on the lookout for spies," the mapmaker warned us.* She stole a glance at Jake on the ground next to her. He tossed and turned. Her mind was full of questions she dared not ask him. *Do they know you're runnin' with us? Is Watson followin' us? What are we gonna do?*

Within the hour, twigs snapped beneath the cottonwood tree. The old man took off running across the field like he knew exactly where he was going. Phoebe noticed he wasn't limping.

Jake nudged her. "Wake Liney up!"

Phoebe shook Liney gently.

"We just lay down," Liney complained.

Phoebe knew her friend had rested poorly for the past three weeks. She had seen her head lifted up, listening long hours for slavecatchers, instead of sleeping.

"That old man was a traitor," Phoebe whispered in Liney's ear. "He didn't know the password and kept askin' us about the underground. By the looks of him, he didn't walk to Alabama all the way from Florida, either."

Liney rubbed her eyes but did not get up.

"They're on Jake's trail. They found the blood!" Phoebe yanked Liney to her feet. It was as if a drum beat in Phoebe's mind. *Slavecatchers, slavecatchers*, it drummed.

"What are we gonna do, Jake?" Dark circles ringed Liney's eyes.

From the ground, Sarah stared at her mother with wide eyes, questions suspended on her lips.

"Move on. Stay in the water until we find the big lake. After that, there'll be deep swamp no one will chase us through."

Phoebe stood up tall. She placed her empty backpack on her back, then swung Bethy onto her shoulders.

"I'm packed. Let's go."

A half-smile flitted across Jake's face. "You sure make me laugh, Phoebe. You look like a young colt ready for a race."

"Time enough to laugh when we're safe," bossed Liney. "Let's run!"

Jake took the lead. Phoebe's feet hit the water with a thud. She balanced over stones and the mud river bottom without lifting her feet to make a splash. She only looked straight ahead, scouting for the big lake. But

Liney kept twisting her head behind them to check.

The sun lit up everything diamond sharp. It gleamed on Jake's dark hair and skin. For the first time Phoebe saw him in bright sunlight. His square chin and full lips. His face smooth except for the hint of hair above his lips. He was somewhere between a boy and a man. She longed to touch his face, to stop for a single moment just to look at him and feel him look at her. *If we ever reach a safe place*, she promised, *I'll come close to you. I will run forever until we find it.* Phoebe's feet pounded over the rocks, running past Jake, on and on. She thought she heard the barking of bloodhounds and once a boom of gunshot. It all seemed part of the rushing stream. She did not stop to listen to it.

Move fast. Be strong. Become the water and float over these rocks. Swirl around them. Disappear.

The water rose waist deep, higher and higher, almost swallowing her. Phoebe's feet no longer touched the ground. She pushed Bethy as high up on her shoulders as she could, then spread her arms wide and swam into the deep waters. She beat her arms with the fury of wings.

Soon they would rest in the swamp. Soon they would be safe. Jake had promised her and that was enough.

Sometimes I Feel Like a Motherless Child

They headed north into the swamp that leaked out of Weiss Lake. Sounds broke into the stillness of Phoebe's mind like a sudden splash on the surface of calm lake water. Hounds barked in the distance. Men yelled. Phoebe knew she had not imagined it before. All afternoon, they had been followed. Slavecatchers or soldiers, they did not know which, led by an old slave's words.

When they reached the swamp, it was not yet dark and they could still be seen. There was no clear path through it. Tree trunks stood bare with one branch pointing the way. Rotting logs lay like dead bodies. Branches dropped to the ground with a single touch. Everywhere was the smell of decay.

If only night would come, they cannot follow us here into the deep of this swamp. Darkness will swallow us whole. The men may not have light with them for a night chase.

Light! Phoebe suddenly remembered how Liney got caught. The glow of a pine torch had followed her. Slavecatchers had held it high, searching in the night, finding her, lighting her up. Their knife had gleamed, coming closer and closer. It sliced through her friend's tongue. Phoebe stole a glance behind her. Liney ran with her head twisted backward. Her children, thin and unfed, were clutched in her arms.

Remembering. Always remembering.

There was a rush all around them. Unspoken thoughts swirled around them like wind. The children's cries froze upon their lips. An awful smell of sweat and fear rose from their flesh.

Phoebe had not slept for two days. Numbness hugged her bones yet she concentrated on what the mapmaker said. "Time stands still in the swamp and hides you. But you're likely to get lost in it."

Hide us now, she prayed. Praying words filled her mind until there was no space left for any other thoughts.

Her breath came in gasps. *Bring the darkness on*, her footsteps beat out a rhythm. *Drop us deep into shadow.* Ahead of her, Jake cut his way through the dim swamp. He circled tree trunks with his hands. Phoebe recalled Old Willie's words about moss on trees pointing north. But moss grew on all sides of these decaying trees. No sign pointed north. Something wanted to keep them lost and forever turning around and around. They were running in circles, running from voices without bodies and bodies without shape. The voices had the white name of fear.

At long last, darkness fell. They were deep inside the swamp by then. The barking faded away. The voices dimmed.

Hide us now, they all chanted silently.

"Stop!" whispered Liney.

They linked hands and paused. Not an animal stirred. Silence. The slavecatchers had given up their search. They carried no light with them. No stars shone the way to anyone. The swamp folded its arms around them. *We are lost*, they realized, *locked like a secret inside this swamp*. Phoebe looked in all directions. Total blackness. A light rain fell. Mosquitoes buzzed in their ears and bit their bare skin. Phoebe shivered in her wet clothes but knew they could not kindle a fire, for that would light the way to them brighter than any pine torch.

Phoebe turned toward Jake. She remembered him high jumping, his legs leaping higher than anyone else's, his landing soft as butter. She was the watcher, the girl on the edge of the circle that surrounded him. She had clapped her hands unseen to the music he jumped to. She waited for his directions now like she had once waited for his high jump. But his face was twisted in pain, a look she had not seen before.

"Slavecatchers with no face!" He shook from head to toe. "I don't know who we're runnin' from. I've seen Watson's face. Master Williams, too. Fat, greedy faces. Countin' how much we're worth."

I hope never to see their faces again, shuddered Phoebe. *Never to come that close!*

"I been spun in too many circles to know which way is

north or south anymore." Jake headed into the swamp alone.

Phoebe rose to follow him but Liney yanked her back.

"Leave him be, girl. A swamp is evil. It puts a spell on you. Jake's walkin' around right now in that spell."

"I could help him. Let me go."

"Give him time. Let me catch my breath and . . ."

We can't stay here. There's nothin' to do here, Phoebe panicked, *except sit and wait for slavecatchers to grab us.*

"What . . . whatever can we do here?"

"Sleep," sighed Liney. "If we don't catch a few hours rest now, we'll never outrun those slavecatchers come morning."

"We're in danger, Liney!" Phoebe spoke sharply. "Don't sleep!"

"Momma, when we gonna stop?" begged Sarah.

"I'm hungry!" Bethy tugged on Phoebe's pants.

Phoebe dug her hand deep into the backpack. Too late she remembered there was no food inside, not even a crumb. Bethy stared at Phoebe's empty hands. Huge tears flooded her face and then she broke into deep sobs. Suddenly the child lost her breath, startling them all.

"There now, child. Got yourself all upset!" Liney patted her back. "Come to momma, now."

Bethy ran into her arms, gasping for air, until she caught her breath. At last she shut her eyes. Her sister sighed and lay down quietly on her mother's lap. Liney gathered both children on top her chest, trying to warm them through all their wet clothing, as she leaned against a tree. Phoebe's eyes felt heavy. *We must not all sleep or we'll be discovered by the slavecatchers. If the children sleep, they will forget their hunger. Liney, too, is draggin' herself. Jake left us alone. He trusts me to keep guard.*

Phoebe squatted on her heels to stay awake. Her stomach ached and grumbled. She stared into the darkness. Her thoughts shifted back and forth like shadows from present to past. She saw her father sitting on the back porch evenings, waiting for her to come home. His face was full of deep lines she did not remember, each one like a whip burn on her heart. The moon rose and fell and still he did not sleep.

I couldn't tell you my secret, she confessed. *Didn't know where I was goin'. Followin' a dream, grandpa's and Rachel's. Was it yours, too? You told me we'd be lost without our dreams. But you never followed yours. You wanted me to stay put, be safe, hold fast. But something called me, like it did Rachel. We just had to go without you. Forgive us, Papa.*

In the quiet night, an owl hooted. Phoebe jerked herself awake. Memory tears wet her cheeks. No sign of Jake. Liney slept on. Then she heard it — brush breaking ahead. Her hand flew to shake Liney but froze in midair. If it were slavecatchers passing, the children might alert everyone with their waking cries. She hunched on her heels and whispered to her heart to stay still.

Tree branches parted. A herd of deer appeared, the color of winter brush, bone-bleached gray, invisible. They fed with their heads tugging at the earth, standing in the dark meadow. One lifted its head, following Phoebe's scent on the air, until its brown eyes fell upon hers. For long minutes it stared. *Hidin' all day. Creepin' out at dusk. Never safe. Always hungry. Full of secrets and fear, just like me.* The herd shifted back into the swamp like dream shadows.

Phoebe crawled into the meadow, searching until she found the deer's food. Even in the darkness, she knew it. Crisp watercress growing without sun. It would keep them alive. She stuffed her backpack full with it.

"Breakfast!" Phoebe rocked Liney awake.

The four runaways chewed in silence. The watercress tasted as bittersharp as grass. No one complained. Moments later, Phoebe heard Jake's footsteps touch the ground soft and smooth as butter.

"See a way out, Jake?" Liney handed him the fresh herbs.

"This swamp stretches for miles. I can't light a torch to look ahead. No use killin' game because we can't build a fire to cook it. We gotta move on. Those men will search for us come morning."

"Which way is north?" Phoebe blurted out.

"My insides tell me to go this way." Jake pointed to a grove of dead trees. "I got no facts to prove it. If it were just me lost, I wouldn't care. But, I don't want to lead you the wrong way."

Jake dug his hands into his pockets and frowned.

Liney placed a hand on his shoulder. "You been leadin' us fine. We gotta move. Folks livin' here must know how to get in and out of this swamp. They'll show the way to the slavecatchers."

Phoebe watched Jake. Something in his eyes leaped, flame by flame into fire, wild and bright. *Answers!*

"Let's go." He lifted Bethy onto his shoulders. She clung to his neck as if he'd been long gone. "I missed you too, child. I'm never gonna leave you again. Gotta stick together."

They walked in the dark until there was a change. A pink glow lit the right half of the sky. They remembered Amos' map. "Sunrise to your right. Head northeast." They were going the right way. The cold mountains lay dead ahead.

Phoebe's feet pounded the earth swift and hard.

Cover us in mountains and shadow no white man will travel through. We are runnin' fast again. Runnin' ahead to the dreamplace. One mind. One memory. All of us are stickin' together.

River Ride

In the Smoky Mountains, they hiked the ridge trails, paths only deer trod on. The high peaks looked down on them, silently watching. The runaways spent weeks climbing and slipping on rocks, their legs growing lean and taut. Mist and shadow swallowed them. At night, dampness seeped through their clothes, chilling them, setting Phoebe to coughing. She felt a heaviness in her chest, the cool mountain air stinging sharply in her lungs. They pushed on. Cougar footprints. Coyote droppings. Predators who never showed themselves but whom Phoebe sensed stalking them. The runaways grabbed berries dried on bushes, cracked hickory nuts open with rocks, and gulped handfuls of ice-cold spring water. By the time the mountains led due east, it was mid-October. They headed down.

They followed streams that trickled out of the mountains on and on, as they turned into little rivers. Another week passed. They stayed in the woods, away from any town. They did not meet a single person. At last, they saw a wide river. They crept to the riverbank and followed it along. The land rose high on both sides again. They finally reached the Kentucky River.

Some nights later as they were wading through the river, they heard a call up ahead. "Whoo! Whoo! Whoo!" It was the call Phoebe learned years ago. "That signal may save your life one day. Be a conductor callin' you, soundin' like an owl," Old Willie's words reminded her. She listened quietly, her body leaning into the wind. In one second, the time it took for sound to travel from her ear to her soul, Phoebe decided it was no hoot owl calling. She edged forward.

Jake hid Liney and the children in bull rushes and crawled behind Phoebe. For long minutes all they heard was water splashing against shore. The hoots loudened. A lantern blinked one blue light, followed by one yellow light. Over and over. The river signals. Phoebe raced ahead, Jake fast at her heels.

A ferryboat waited around a bend of the river.

"Who's there?" a boatman challenged them.

"We are lost, sir," Phoebe called back in the dark.

"How many?"

"Five!" Jake stepped beside her, a lantern lighting their faces.

"You are found! Not a moment too soon. Just about ready to sail. Not safe to be stopping. Get aboard for the Ohio River."

Jake turned and signaled Liney with owl hoots. She

soon joined them at the boat with Bethy and Sarah. Jake scooped the children in his arms. Everyone boarded the boat. Steam pumped out of its smokestack like a hot spring. Men led them below into the storeroom.

Phoebe sighed at the unexpected warmth and collapsed on top some grain sacks strewn over the floor. *Onboard for the Ohio River!* Her eyes shut against the night. She felt Bethy snuggle beside her. Beneath her, waves lapped back and forth. The engine purred steadily away. After a while, Phoebe did not even remember how she got onboard. Her legs felt like heavy weights. Her body sank deeper and deeper. She coughed in fits, squeezing her mouth into a nearby sack to soften the sound.

Somewhere Jake was talking to the boatmen. "A short journey ahead," she overheard. Somewhere Sarah was asking Liney a million questions. "Gonna get there real soon? Gonna find a soft white bed?" And Liney was whispering answers, "Soon enough, child! Soon enough!"

Phoebe drifted with the water, downriver, down and down the Kentucky River toward the one river: the Ohio River. It was the river all slaves knew about, the river of dreams. A wide river running along the edge of Ohio, like a borderguard between slave states and freedom states.

Carry me. Carry me. I can't run anymore, she sighed. *Lift me. Lift me. I can't fly anymore.* In her dreams, she stood on a cliff in the white dress. She jumped up to fly but fell back down to the ground. Her wings were folded flat against her body, unable to open.

Two nights later, the boat stopped. An anchor

splashed overboard. The boatmen signaled with one blue and one yellow flash of the lantern. A foghorn blew, deep and low, close by.

"A steamboat's comin' up the Ohio. Climb inside these."

The slaves slipped inside brown burlap potato sacks. Phoebe wrapped her arms around Bethy to cushion her. A steamboat halted alongside the ferry.

"Any freight?" the captain yelled down to them.

The sacks lay flat and still onboard.

"Three sacks of potatoes," shouted the boatman. "Grown down South. Drop off before Ripley."

"Heave them up!"

Several white men stood onboard watching from the deck, their breath blowing smoke clouds in the night air. They wrapped their coats around their bodies and walked away. The sacks were tossed upon the deck and carried below. For hours they drifted, lying on the ship's bottom. The boat rocked them back and forth. The whole world seemed upside down to Phoebe. She was glad for once that her stomach was empty.

Late that night, candlelight filled the hold. The runaways burrowed into their sacks. Footsteps crept closer. Someone reached out and loosened the sacks.

A voice whispered to them, "Come on out."

Phoebe stuck her head out. In the dimness stood an old man, his skin weathered like driftwood, staring straight down at her. In his hands, he held some food.

"Aye. It's safe enough, poor souls."

They sat up and ate the man's sourdough bread and sausage.

"I am the ship's steward. Captain put me in charge of runaways. Used to be you could ride this whole river safely. But every slavecatcher knows about the Ohio now. Slaves been traveling on it too long." The old man shook his head sadly. "Even at night, patrols are stationed on Ohio riverbanks, watching for slaves swimming across."

"Which way do we head, steward?" asked Jake.

The old man held his palm out flat before their eyes. He pointed to the hundred lines that crisscrossed it, deep and long. Sarah tunneled out of her sack to see.

"There's as many paths across this here state as there are lines on my palm. Stations right straight up in Ohio. Quakers all along. What port do you plan on heading to?"

Phoebe remembered the word sounded like darkness and sand.

"Sandy . . . dark . . . dusk?" she hesitated.

"Sandusky!" screamed Sarah.

"Don't say that word aloud," warned the steward. "Conductors call it a code word, Sunrise. Slaves stand on the shore of Lake Erie looking across to freedom rising on the other side — Canada."

Phoebe was wide awake now. Her head had cleared when the steward mentioned Canada. *Promised land, my grandpa believed. It's called Sunrise.* She pictured landing on the shore of Lake Erie, watching the sun rise up in Canada where freedom was. *It'll be so bright, shining on that white land.* She felt ready to run again.

Jake questioned the steward again. "What's our first stop?"

"Ripley Station. Look for a house high on a bluff over the river. Wide porch. Four pine trees. If you find it, there will be rest and shelter for the night.

"Steward," begged Liney, "how will we know what to do then?"

"After you leave Ripley Station, follow the Ohio until you see a narrow river heading north. That's the Scioto. Aim due north. Be on the lookout for camps there. Some are slavecatchers. But the Union army is there, too. They'll help you out."

Above their heads, a foghorn blew three times. Warning!

"Plenty more I could tell you but there's no time left. Hide in those sacks. I'll throw you ashore just before Ripley. Not safe to drop you near the station. Too many eyes watching. This underground runs on secrecy. Got to keep it that way."

The boat slowed down but did not stop. First one sack, then another was thrown onshore in the dark. Men's voices echoed across the water. Passengers walked the decks. The steward complained loudly that no one was on hand to pick up their cargo. The first two sacks hit the ground hard. Then the last sack with Phoebe and Bethy inside was tossed in the air high above the dark waters. It landed a distance downstream.

The steamboat sailed on into the cold Ohio night.

CHAPTER TWENTY

Ripley Station

Ohio was free land. Cold, hard earth beneath her feet that hummed a rhythm. To Phoebe, it was the rhythm of freedom. She felt light as a breeze and flew along the shore searching for the first station in a free state.

"A house high on a bluff with four pine trees," she remembered the steward's words. *Long-awaited rest!*

They saw no houses for an hour. They waded silently in the swirling river, soaked from their feet to their waist. Late that night, they passed one white house high on the bank. Wooden stairs led up to it from the river. The runaways tiptoed up the steps and gathered around the house. A candle shone upstairs but it was so dark, they couldn't see how many trees there were or what kind. Through the windows of the parlor, they saw a party of twenty people inside. Laughter sparked on the cold night air.

The front door opened wide.

"Goodnight, folks. I'll see you tomorrow morning for services," said a woman in a long black skirt and neat bonnet.

As the woman stood in the doorway, Phoebe caught a glimpse of the parlor with a hearth fire burning, red and warm against the cool night. Phoebe wished this were the place. A cough struggled to rise up out of her chest. They had slept in the damp woods and waded in rivers too many nights. No matter how tightly she wrapped her coat around her, the chill drilled deep down to her bones and set her teeth chattering.

Liney frowned. They had only stopped at quiet places before, cabins in deep woods and old barns.

"Let's move on!" she muttered.

Bethy yanked on her pant leg. She would whine and cry herself to sleep again tonight if she were not fed. So many times on their journey, she had gone to sleep with an empty belly.

"Why would she shine a candle upstairs," argued Phoebe, "if she's stayin' downstairs? Must be a signal. Let's find out!"

"Let's just knock on the door," Jake agreed. "Tell her we're hungry. If it's not the station, we'll move on fast."

"Too risky," warned Liney. "She'll be frightened by the looks of us and run for the sheriff. Besides, someone may still be inside."

Bethy yanked again on Liney's pant leg. Jake scowled. He sprang off his heels and crept toward the house, crouching by each window until lights dimmed in the parlor.

"She's alone," he reported back to them. "There's chicken on the counter and milk, too. We gotta risk it, Liney."

Liney tightened her jaw and looked from Jake to Phoebe. They both leaned toward the house.

"Momma!" echoed Sarah. "Let's go in!"

"Maybe I been runnin' too long. Scared for longer than not. Hidin' all this time and movin' in the dark. Can't trust a white face."

"We're all tired of runnin', Liney." Jake reasoned. "Tired of not eatin' enough, too."

"We got a tip to come here by a conductor," Phoebe reminded her. "Whites chained us in slavery but some are settin' us free. Eda. The mapmaker. Ferrymen. The steward. Maybe this woman, too."

Liney sighed deeply as if a weight fell from her shoulders, the weight of hiding and running too long. "You two go ahead and knock," she decided. "We'll hide here."

Sarah edged near Phoebe but her mother yanked her back.

"You sure, Liney?" Phoebe begged her friend.

"Sure enough. I'll wait for your signal. Go on."

Sarah's eyes shone bright with tears. Phoebe knew she could not risk taking the child with her. Jake grabbed her hand and they raced to the front door. One hard knock. One soft one. Three times. Footsteps rushed inside. Then a flicker of candlelight appeared. The woman opened the door wide, her face flushed from running.

"Ma'am," begged Jake with his hat in his hands, "we

are tired and hungry. Can you give us a meal?"

The woman peered at them with narrowed eyes. "Are you alone?"

"Just us two here," answered Jake.

"Did anyone follow you?"

"Haven't seen a soul for weeks."

A long pause. The woman raised her candle higher to study them.

"Where are you coming from?"

"Come from the river, ma'am . . . we're lost!" Phoebe suddenly remembered the password.

The woman opened the door wide and smiled. "You are found!"

The heat of the fire hit Phoebe in the face like warm hands touching her. Something inside her melted down with the white light feeling of being in a free state.

Oh free-dom! When I am free! The words sprang to her mind. *And be-fo' I'd be a slave, I'll be free-dom o-ver me!*

Sweet words sung on a forever hot day in the fields.

"You've reached Ripley Station." The woman led them into the kitchen and placed fat drumsticks on two plates. The smell of warm meat made Phoebe's stomach growl.

"There's three more of us outside, ma'am," Jake blurted out.

The woman nodded. "Bring them in."

She set down three more plates. Just as Jake rose to get Liney, she and her children appeared in the kitchen doorway, wide-eyed at the warmth. Everyone ate their fill. Bethy almost chewed her drumstick in one bite, bone and meat together, until Liney grabbed the bone. Sarah gulped glass after glass of cold milk, not even breathing between swallows.

"Eat slow, girls! Gonna make yourself sick," Liney cautioned. "Your bellies empty so long don't know what real food is anymore."

When the girls finally settled onto Liney's lap, licking their greasy fingers, the woman spoke. She was the widow Rankins. Her husband had been the town's clergyman before he died.

"Praise to the Lord you have made it halfway to Canada. Many are the slaves who do not," she told them. "For years a candle has burned in my upstairs window every night to lead your kind to this house. It's a signal we use for safe stations in Ohio. But slavecatchers roam through here now. Last time I sheltered runaways was two months ago when a family of slaves from Alabama stayed here."

Phoebe shot a quick look at her friends. "How many slaves were there?" she asked.

"Five," the widow recalled. "A family of three started off together. But two more joined up later. They were running in a pack."

"Do you remember the ones who joined up?" Phoebe asked.

Mrs. Rankins nodded. "They are clear in my mind. So young. A girl and a boy. About fifteen, I'd say. Seemed to be in love. That girl was tall and pretty, too. The longest braids I ever saw."

Phoebe sat straight up. Her heart pounded. "Did she

say her name?"

"Best no one tells me their name. Then I don't have to lie if someone comes looking for them. But that family must almost be in Canada now."

Phoebe stared at her friends. She knew what they were thinking. *Rachel was here! She's alive. She's safe. She may still be on the underground trail.* She couldn't help but smile to think she was staying at the same station where her sister had stayed.

Mrs. Rankins pushed back her chair and walked over to a closet in the hall. She handed them clean towels, blankets, and pillows. "Tonight, you'll wash your bodies and your clothes and then rest up in the attic. Tomorrow night you'll run again but the chill will be off your bones."

Later, when they walked into the bathroom, Phoebe gasped. Reflected in the mirror were her face and Liney's, two thin faces smeared with dirt, dressed in muddy clothes, with only the whites of their eyes shining. They looked like strangers. Phoebe removed her cap. Her greasy hair clung to her scalp. She had forgotten what she looked like, forgotten she even had braids or was a young woman.

"Is this what we look like?" Phoebe shook with laughter.

Liney grinned and threw a washcloth at her. They scrubbed the children in a basin, dressed them in woolen nightshirts, and combed their hair out before they ran up into the attic to play with Jake.

"You may run around tonight and keep your candle lit. But come day, you must be still as mice," the widow warned the girls. "Those floorboards creak and no one must know you are up there."

High above them they heard giggles, the pitter-patter of footsteps chasing one another, and the thump of pillows flying in the air.

"Bethy and Sarah must think they're already in Canada, what with all those pillows and blankets!" Liney exclaimed with a bright face. "Just like I promised them."

"Sure feels like freedom to me, too!" smiled Phoebe. She stood still, watching her friend wash their clothes.

Liney looked just like she did when they first met, strong and straight. But whipping had worn her down. She had become thin, too, from all the running and not eating enough. *For this one night, we will get a taste of Freedom Land. You will feel like the African princess I imagined you to be.*

Phoebe touched Liney's arm. "I always wanted to tell you why I came with you. I saw you in my dreams. Almost from the first, you were flyin' right beside me."

"How did you know it was me, girl?" Liney smiled back at her.

"When I first met you, pickin' so strong, you reminded me of an African princess. Sun for your crown. That's how you shone in my dreams, too. If it weren't for meetin' you, I may never have dreamed about the underground."

"All I did was talk is all," protested Liney. "I didn't have dreams like you."

"But you wanted to run. That made me want it, too."

The two friends hugged and Liney wrung out their

wet clothes. Then it was Phoebe's turn to bathe. For the first time in her life, Phoebe soaked in a tub of hot water, which touched her skin like silk. She washed her hair with store-bought soap. A scent of roses filled the air. As she dried herself in front of the mirror, her body looked inches taller than when she left Alabama. She was surprised to see her thin waist and breasts swelling on her chest and how her hips were beginning to round. Her hair, when combed out, touched her shoulder blades in thick black waves.

Phoebe slipped into a white cotton nightgown. It trailed on the floor behind her, the softest thing she had ever felt next to her skin. She tiptoed into the attic with her candle held high. *Will Jake be waiting to see me? Will he notice how I've changed tonight?* She remembered the cellar where she met him. The attic, too, was full of shadows that shifted with the candlelight, but it was dry and high, warm with candlelight. The pine floorboards creaked as she pressed her bare feet over them.

Jake turned her way and the children stopped running to watch Phoebe climb into the attic. "We are halfway to freedom," she announced to them. "I keep dreamin' I can fly there."

Phoebe closed her eyes. She lifted the hem of her nightgown and twirled in a circle. Rows of cotton stretched far below her, white and untouched as clouds. She danced high above them in the sky, wearing the white cotton dress that spread out from her body like wings. She sang aloud.

If I just had two wings,
bright an-gels a-bove,
I would fly a-way to the king-dom,
bright an-gels a-bove!

"Dance with me, child." She swung Bethy up high until her head almost touched the shadowy rafters.

"I never told you about the white dress, the one I dreamt about before we left the plantation. This must be that dress! I dreamt that when I wore it, I could fly high above the cotton fields, away from slavery."

Phoebe swirled her skirt hem up into the air and twirled in circles with Bethy in her arms.

"Lift me up!" Sarah screamed. "I wanna fly to the clouds!"

The wooden floorboards shook. Jake rose from the shadows and lifted Sarah up. The girls screeched and giggled as Jake and Phoebe lowered them down to the floor and then lifted them up high to the ceiling, light as birds in their arms. They laughed until their bellies ached. Finally they set the children down upon the soft blankets. The girls propped themselves up to watch Jake and Phoebe.

Phoebe reached up and touched his face for a moment. *A safe place at last*, she remembered her promise. *I'll come close to you.* He held her hands and spun her in circles around and around. He twirled her faster and faster. Her nightgown spun in an arc of white light. Then suddenly he stopped and hugged her closely. His chest next to hers felt leaner than Phoebe had imagined it would until she remembered that no one had eaten much on this trip.

He looked into her eyes. "You smell like roses, Phoebe."

Jake and Phoebe danced on while Bethy and Sarah curled up on the blankets, yawning, full of food and dance and flying high in the attic.

Liney laughed as she climbed upstairs with a laundry basket full of wet clothes.

"I thought everyone was tired from all the runnin'!"

Phoebe blushed. She stopped dancing and let go of Jake's hand. She ran over to help her friend hang the wet clothes across the rafters.

"Oh, Liney, we're dancin' to freedom. Look at those children's faces. They never looked so happy. All of us are gettin' closer to Canada." The words burst out of Phoebe like a song.

Liney leaned forward to examine Phoebe's flushed face. "You changin', girl. Yesterday, you looked like a muskrat dragged out of the river. Tonight you becomin' something beautiful right before my eyes . . . Now, let's get some sleep. We all got feather covers and pillows just like in Freedom Land. Toasty warm, too."

Liney snuffed the candle out. Phoebe lay her head on a soft pillow. In the darkness, she braided Bethy's hair. "Goodnight, Jake," she said. "Thanks for leadin' us on."

"You're the one runnin' so fast, hard to keep up with you," Jake whispered in the dark, beside her. "I remember when we were searchin' for the big lake. Just when I thought it's never gonna come soon enough, you spread out your arms to swim like you did tonight when you were dancin'. Like you knew it was there all along."

Phoebe fell asleep that night with a smile. In her dreams, she saw herself spinning in the white dress. Her dress flowed around her hips like water. Waves of black hair flew all around her. She twirled so fast that everything around her became a blur. Tiny white specks flew from the sky and covered her with white light.

CHAPTER
TWENTY-ONE

Riding the Ohio

Mrs. Rankins gave them woolen jackets the next evening, just before they left. "The Ohio runs deep and wide here. You need to build a raft soon. Look for the Scioto River. It breaks off from the Ohio, heading north. It's a few nights' journey ahead. Safe stations are up and down it. You'll see their candles burning from the river. One's at Waverly, two hours upstream from the mouth of the Scioto."

Jake's hand held Phoebe's when they slipped out of the back door. His hand guided her as they skimmed down the wooden steps back to the river. His hand steadied her underwater as their bodies were swallowed beneath the river one by one, walking upstream, the current pushing back hard against them, full with November rain. The children rode high on their shoulders. Liney paced a footstep behind. Together, it was as if a rope was tied to all of them, holding them steady.

That night, the Ohio deepened, circling their knees one moment, then rising up past their chests. It was time to build a raft and ride its back. They hunted by the riverbank but found only rotten branches instead of dry timber. They remembered the mapmaker had told them to search inside old barns for logs.

One rainy morning Jake returned from his scouting, his shoulders hunched together. Raw wind blasted from the north.

"There's an empty barn beyond this field," he shivered. "Seems deserted. Let's rest awhile there. Got a hayloft to sleep in. Full of logs and thick rope, too. Tonight, I'll build the raft and we'll sail on."

Liney nodded wearily. Their clothes were soaked through to their flesh. All night long, the river wind had blown so coldly at their backs that Bethy's teeth still chattered. Her mouth set in a straight line and she was suddenly quiet. Phoebe coughed for hours without stopping. She felt like a sleepwalker, sleeping while awake, unable to sleep when they stopped. She tossed and turned with an empty belly, always alert.

The friends crept through the field and slipped into the barn. Inside, it was dry and quiet. Dim. They climbed straight up the ladder to a loft and buried themselves deep in hay. Instantly, they fell asleep. The wind rose and the barn shuddered but they did not hear it.

That evening, Jake laid out logs on the floor and tied them together with the thick rope he had found. By midnight, the raft was ready. It was eight feet by eight feet, flat and lightweight. He yanked two flat planks down from the side of the barn that they could use for paddles. *Tap! Tap! Tap!* Something hit the tin roof above their heads. Liney peered outside through a crack in the wall. White balls of ice hit the barn hard. Hail!

"Something's shootin' at us!" Sarah piped up. "Cold and white. What are we gonna do?"

"We can't leave tonight!" Liney's thin face was so pinched with worry, she looked years older. "We haven't dried out yet. Let's leave in the morning."

"We can't travel in the morning light," insisted Jake. "We'll certainly be seen if we lug this raft across the field in full daylight. We gotta slip away now!"

Phoebe's eyes shut. She pushed down a deep cough. She longed to sleep forever and did not know how she could stand up and push her legs to walk on again. All her dreampower seemed to have vanished. Bethy slumped heavily against her as if agreeing.

"This here's a quiet place." Liney felt Bethy's forehead. It was hot. "We could use a rest. Stay out of this storm. No one came in durin' the day while we were sleepin'. Maybe no one uses this barn. We'll run out before dawn. No one will know we've been here."

"Alright. No use arguin'," muttered Jake. "Let's stay."

Phoebe leaned against Jake's shoulder, half asleep. He wrapped his arms snugly around her. They slept in fits that night, knowing they must awaken early. Once, Phoebe awoke in dead darkness and listened to freezing rain hit against the roof. Her heart raced in her chest and she did not know why.

Early the next morning, the women climbed down the

ladder with the children. Jake was still asleep in the loft above. Liney gathered their coats that had dried a little overnight. Sarah was playing with a strand of hay on the floor, singing to herself, when the barn door creaked wide open. The child froze like a statue. Phoebe and Liney backed into the shadows, pulling Bethy with them.

A white farmer stood in the gray morning light, looking in. He walked over to the log pile. Phoebe held her breath. Seconds passed. Sarah sneezed in the sudden draft from the open barn door.

The man turned in surprise and headed straight toward the child. "Who do you belong to?"

Sarah's mouth opened wide to scream but no sound came out.

"She belongs to me and no one else." Liney marched out of the shadows and lifted Sarah up.

"You spend the night here?" he sneered. "Up in the loft?"

"No!" Phoebe yelled, pushing Bethy deeper into the shadows behind her. "We slept down here, just us three. We won't bother you no more. We're on our way out."

Phoebe stepped an inch nearer the door.

"No, you don't, girl. You're worth money to me." The man suddenly lunged at Phoebe and twisted her arm behind her back. "Slavecatchers are in my house right now searching for your kind. Won't they be pleased!"

Pieces of hay sifted down from the loft behind the man's head. Up in the loft, Jake was awake. He was moving. Phoebe felt it with a shiver down her spine.

"What are you gonna do, sir?" she asked, trying to

stall for time. The man twisted her arm harder and harder, making her gasp.

His hot breath touched her cheek. "Tie you up, then call the slavecatchers. Collect my reward," he chuckled and dragged her into a horse stall. He glared at Liney clutching Sarah. "If one of you makes a move to stop me, I'll smack you so hard, you won't get up again."

He slammed Phoebe against the stall. "Where's my rope?"

In a flash, Jake jumped down from the loft and landed with a thud upon the man's shoulders. Phoebe fell back. The two men rolled over the floor in a blur of bodies. Straw flew in all directions. The white man squeezed Jake's neck between his hands but Jake wrenched free. He dove on top of the man and banged his head hard against a board. The man lay still.

"When he comes to," Jake spat, wiping blood from his lips, "he'll run to get the slavecatchers."

"Let's get out of here!" Liney ran toward the door and peeked out. The children clung to her pant leg. Bethy lifted up her arms to be held.

Phoebe and Jake carried the raft to the river and they all boarded it. Liney lay flat down with her children. Jake pushed off. Side by side, he and Phoebe paddled. They skimmed the river's back high and dry. They flew over it. It was not the trip Phoebe imagined, riding swift on the Ohio, sailing ahead to freedom in the safety of the dark. Her heart beat in her throat, and waves of sweat flushed her body in spite of the cold. Then the sun rose and lit them up, bright as targets. They desperately eyed the passing land for a place to hide.

At last they saw an old wooden shed far off in a corn-field. They dragged the raft out of the water and across the field and hid it in the shed. Soon they all squatted inside, breathless. Bethy collapsed in a quiet heap on Liney's lap while her sister squirmed for a while. Liney grabbed pieces of dried corn scattered in the field. Sarah sucked them with a squeezed-up face. Finally she lay down.

The three friends sat up and faced one another as they had in the cellar months ago, watching silently, listening still. There was a thinness to them now, a bone leanness. Their coats were mud stained and raggedy. Even their faces looked old, as if they had always been runaway slaves.

"Slavecatchers!" whispered Phoebe. "They're chasin' us again. Wonder if it's the ones from the swamp?"

Liney frowned. Her eyes traced the high cheekbones on Phoebe's flushed face. She leaned toward Phoebe and whispered in her ear. "How much did Williams want for me?"

"Why I . . . I don't remember. Seems so long ago."

Liney's slanted eyes bored straight into hers.

"Remember."

Phoebe remembered the Alabama morning clear and bright in her mind when she had spied on the three white men, the voice of the fat white Master cutting into her ears. "If you're willin' to pay one thousand for her, Watson, she's yours."

"Tell me!" Liney turned Phoebe's chin and forced her

to look into her eyes.

Phoebe murmured, "A thousand."

"So . . . it's me they want!" Liney's jaw dropped. "Probably set a big bounty on my head. I already tried runnin' before — I'm the one they wanna go after. I should let 'em have me, get 'em off your trail. They'd leave you alone then. Look at us hidin' like animals in a trap."

"Don't say that, Liney. We all gotta stick together. We're family."

As soon as the words were out of her mouth, Phoebe felt a stabbing pain in her belly and doubled over. *Those were the words my father once said! 'Not for a family!' he warned me. Now we are far from him, far from safety. Danger is everywhere. There is no one to help us.*

Jake suddenly stood up. His face was twisted, dark and long.

"Watson's behind this. I read him like white folks do a book. He owned me, every inch of me. He won't give up 'til he gets me. You heard that Confederate soldier back near Montgomery." Jake touched his leg where the spear of the gun had pierced him two months ago. "There's a fat reward out for me. If anyone's gotta run back, I'm the one!"

Phoebe's eyes shot back and forth between her two friends. "We been gettin' closer to Canada every day. Just gotta go back to that river right now."

"We have to stay put 'til night," argued Jake. "If we are seen in daylight, they'll grab us for sure."

"We can't just sit here and wait," Phoebe insisted.

"We can move faster on the river." *Maybe we'll stop fightin' there.*

Liney shook her head. "Girl, we are stuck. Can't ride on. But hidin' here gives me the shivers. Feels like a trap."

"We're gonna stay put right here!" Jake slammed his fist into the ground with each word, then buried his head in his hands. "Been all my fault. When we met up, I said I'd run with you. Turns out I'm a noose around your necks, draggin' you back to slavery."

"No!" Phoebe clutched Jake's hand wildly, drawing him into her arms.

"Shush up!" Liney's eyes flashed. "No one's supposed to know we're here."

Jake loosened himself from Phoebe's arms. "Go to sleep now. I'll keep watch. No matter what happens, stick by Liney," he told her.

The women huddled beside the children as if their warmth could still their pounding hearts. Phoebe pressed her lips together and looked at Jake one last time. He crouched in the morning light, his body one tight black muscle.

Phoebe willed herself to sleep, to settle into dreams. But, instead, all morning long, she heard the whispers of slavecatchers in her ears like secrets that could not be told.

CHAPTER
TWENTY-TWO

Slavecatchers

Hours later, voices drifted into Phoebe's ears, cutting into her dreamtime. Male voices spoke outside the shed, growing louder and louder. Her eyelids flew open in the bright sun. She did not know if she was dreaming or sleeping until she felt Jake's hand pressing hard upon her shoulder. His eyes shone like two black stones. He reached over to Liney and shook her awake with his finger over his lips.

"We crossed ten miles since this morning," a man's voice panted, "and still no sign of 'em. I'd like to get my hands on that slave who dared touch a poor white farmer!"

Phoebe peered between the slats of wood. Two white men trudged across the cornfield. Their faded gray clothes were streaked with mud. Across their shoulders rested shotguns. Slavecatchers!

"Full daylight now. Must be hidin'. Been tracin' 'em

since we talked to that old slave. Gotta check everywhere. Like that old shed. Looks like the stalks are parted leadin' to it. Let's go see."

Jake leaped away from Phoebe and crouched down by the edge of the shed. He turned back to look at her. His honey-brown eyes reached out like fire burning straight through her. *Remember me. Remember me.* Phoebe tried to pull him back but it was too late. Jake crashed south through the woods like a wild man swinging his arms. The slavecatchers stopped dead. They jerked their guns eye level. Two shots boomed across the empty cornfield.

"Hey!" Jake called to them from the bushes. "You'll never catch me. I can outrun any of you!"

"C'mon! Let's get him first. He's worth plenty. Dead or alive."

Both men joined the chase for Jake, leaving the shed behind. Shots rang out. Voices yelled. Crashing underfoot. Then silence. A long silence that echoed in Phoebe's ears.

"Let's run!" ordered Liney. "He's leadin' 'em away!"

Phoebe's breath slowly leaked out. Her body slumped forward.

"We can't wait for Jake! He's givin' us a chance to run." Liney tugged her sleeve. "Soldiers will march by soon, too. Let's go!"

Liney motioned Phoebe to help her lift the raft but Phoebe did not move. She opened her mouth to speak but her voice seemed frozen. Sarah sat up and watched, biting her lips. Her eyes were fixed on Phoebe's face.

"Girl, snap out of it!" Liney yanked Phoebe hard but

she still didn't budge. "They'll be back for us if they don't catch Jake. We gotta put miles between us and them."

Bethy clung to Phoebe, screaming loudly, "Where's Jake gone?"

Phoebe hugged her. Tears fell down her face and joined the child's. Sarah sprang forward, wrapping her arms around Phoebe. The three of them huddled together as one person.

"How are we gonna go on without Jake?" Phoebe cried out. "We'll never know what happened to him."

"You and me decided to run together," snapped Liney. "Met up with Jake by chance. Maybe that's how we'll meet again. If he outwits those slavecatchers, he'll head straight for the river. We all got the same map printed in our minds."

Only four of us flew in my dream! Phoebe suddenly remembered. *Liney. Sarah. Bethy. Me. One of us was missin': Jake!* The thought sliced through her like a knife wound. She felt like screaming his name across the field. She bit her tongue hard and squeezed Sarah and Bethy to stop herself from calling out. She stared at Liney and remembered how she had picked beside her and wanted to learn everything her friend knew. Now she felt she had learned too much. She thought of home far away and her father's face, scarred by worry. Her parents were miles and miles behind her with two states forever between them. They couldn't help her. It was no use calling after them. *If only Jake was still beside me!*

"I feel lost without Jake. Without my momma and

papa by my side to tell me what to do."

Phoebe sank down onto her knees and began to shiver. At first, she quivered deep inside. Then her shoulders and chest and even her legs trembled. She could not catch her breath. Liney motioned Bethy and Sarah to move to one side. Then she wrapped her strong brown arms around her friend. She rocked her in her arms as if Phoebe were her own child. All the while, she lifted her head high, listening for slavecatchers.

"We come so far and you done so good," Liney reminded her. "Think what Jake would want you to do without him."

Pictures flashed in Phoebe's mind. Jake running fast in the lead, holding Bethy. Jake looking backward to check on her and Liney. Jake signaling them on. "We're all gonna be safe in Canada," he had encouraged them. "No runnin' anymore. No scared looks on these children's faces."

Jake had vanished like Hannah, Jenny, Lucinda, and Isaac. Like Rachel, too. Jake ran so they could head safely to freedom. She was always the one left behind. The last child in her cabin, mourning her sisters and brother, long gone. The girl at the edge of the circle. Unseen. *I'm the one who has to go ahead now. Am I strong enough to go on without them?* she sighed. *They must have thought so, Jake, too.*

She dried Bethy's tears, lifted her off her lap, and raised her high upon her shoulders. She stood pale and shaking in the sunlight. "I'm comin'."

Phoebe's head spun in all directions. She looked out

across the field and no longer remembered the way back to the river. She wished for darkness like a cloak to slip into. She prayed for the stars and the moon and the night to cover the bright blue sky but there was no hiding from it.

The mapmaker warned us to travel only at night. We have never run in daylight before across flat fields where we can be seen. We cannot even lift our heads to see just where it is we are headed.

They began to crawl across the field. They stayed low down. The two children rode on their backs, clinging to their necks. The only sound was the scrape of the raft dragging behind them through the dried corn stalks. *Swish! Swish! Swish!* The sun was bright. As Phoebe looked up at it, she saw the corn stalks flattening as they crawled through them, waving like arms, signaling their presence. She froze, pulling Liney to a stop. The field was silent except for the cries of crows. *Caw! Caw! Caw!* The birds called warnings to them.

They lay on the cold earth, totally still. For an hour, they listened for soldiers, the pounding of boots and shouts, but everything was strangely silent. They could not wait much longer. Each moment meant the slave-catchers could catch up with them. The sun began to dip down in the sky. They crawled in slow motion. Phoebe hoped the river was near. Just as she was starting to wonder if they were moving in circles, they heard water rushing past.

They could not wait until dark. Perhaps the slave-catchers were only minutes behind them. Phoebe sucked in her breath and stepped into the water. It felt colder than it had earlier that morning. *Just this morning!* So much had happened, it felt like days since they had been in the river. Phoebe followed Liney upstream, guiding the raft into deeper water.

But the tears fell anyway and joined the rushing water at Phoebe's feet. The tears flowed back to the South, back home to Jake.

PART THREE

◇

THE WAY NORTH
WINTER

I got two wings for to veil my face.
I got two wings for to fly with.

CHAPTER TWENTY-THREE

Scioto River

They steered their raft east. The sun slowly began to sink. Phoebe paddled into the chilly wind. River dampness drilled through her bones. As they sailed, Phoebe and Liney kept twisting their heads around. Suddenly Liney gasped out loud. Phoebe turned quickly and saw someone in a field by the shore with his hand raised out. But the river swiftly carried them past before they could even react.

At last, the sun set but they didn't dare stop. The girls clung to the raft, hungry and cold. Bethy's face looked flushed and her tiny body shook. As the darkness grew, so did Phoebe's thoughts. *Jake!* She dared not speak of him to Liney. One word might betray them to someone onshore, for sound had a way of traveling over water, of magnifying. She kept her silence as they rode. Her thoughts sunk deep. They weighed down her body like an anchor, making the raft seem harder to push.

Jake, Phoebe whispered across the night waters, *come back!*

She heard his name echo south but she refused to turn around. Ghosts waited there. Guns. The pounding of boots. Soldiers. Slavecatchers. She paddled on. Sarah was wide awake, right beside Phoebe, her eyes huge in her face, watching. No one answered her questions now about what lay ahead. No one spoke at all. Sometimes Phoebe's hand rested on Bethy's shoulder, ready to rock her back into dreams should she awaken, but the child was quiet except for her chest-wrenching coughs. On the other side of the raft, Liney crouched as she paddled in time with her, watching the land drift past.

At last, they turned a bend in the river. Up ahead, the river widened. Currents swirled. The waterway split in two separate directions. A river opened up to the north. The Scioto River! They steered up it. Mrs. Rankins had told them there would be stations dotting the land if they went ashore. "One at Waverly, past the mouth of the Scioto," she had said. But they had forgotten how far it was. The land was dark as they passed by. Not one candle shone to greet them. By dawn the next day, purple clouds blackened the sky. Driving winds twirled their raft in one direction and then another, spinning it backward. Ice-cold rain fell.

"Can't go on!" yelled Liney above the wind. "Let's get out!"

They crept beneath some evergreens where the ground was cushioned with pine needles. Phoebe breathed in the pine-oil scent of the trees. It cooled her lungs like medicine. She choked back the cough that had nagged her for months. *Good at last to rest. No slavecatcher will scout in this drivin' rain.*

All that day, rain hung like a gray sheet, hiding them within the storm. It hid everything except the ache in Phoebe's heart. She remembered Jake lifting Bethy in the swamp, telling her he'd never leave her alone, his honey-brown eyes warm as campfire. *I have lost him forever like all my family. Sold away. One by one.* She pressed her face against the cold wet ground and wept.

All that evening, the storm kept on. They still could not travel. Phoebe slumped against a tree trunk and stared into the rain.

Liney wrapped an arm around her. "You're hurtin' bad. Jake is gone. Long gone. He won't be catchin' up with us now."

"I didn't know him long but . . . I thought he'd stay and guide us all the way."

"I miss him too, girl. He took care of us from the moment we met up."

"I worry about him all the time," Phoebe cried. "What if they caught him? What would they do to him? Teach me to forget."

Liney shrugged her shoulders. "Hmmph . . . not easy!"

"You had someone you loved once . . . a husband."

Liney's eyes met hers. Phoebe had waited long enough to hear Liney's story. Now was time to ask.

"What was his name?"

The question hung suspended in the air.

"Henry," sighed Liney at long last.

She was silent for so long afterward that Phoebe thought she would not hear more.

"You never seen a man like him," Liney confessed. "Ebony-skinned. Straight as a tree. There was a time when I thought he'd come back, just show up across a row of sea-island cotton. But he never did. I don't even know if he's alive. He's livin' in danger if he is."

"Why is that?"

"He was a conductor on the underground." Tears filled Liney's eyes. "Master came lookin' for him in our cabin and I put up a big fuss. Got whipped hard for it. Gave Henry time to get away."

"What happened after?" Phoebe leaned against Liney.

"They sold me and the girls. Whenever a new owner heard about Henry, he auctioned us off again. I couldn't bear to be sold one more time. Williams found out, too. That's why he wanted to get rid of me. Figured I knew something about the underground but I didn't."

"Didn't Henry tell you all about the underground road?"

Liney shook her head. "Henry wanted me to stay put. My girls were so little then. I couldn't run with babies. They might not make it, he warned me. Begged me to wait a little longer."

If Williams knew about Liney's past, so did my momma, Phoebe realized. *House slaves know everything. No secrets in the big house. Servants listen close.* "Troublemaker," she had called Liney. *My momma thought Liney was dangerous but Liney was just hurtin'.*

"Henry told me to forget him. 'You never had a husband,' he said. I promised not to speak his name. Doesn't mean I don't cry when I think I'll never know where he's at. Did he get safe to the North or is he runnin' back and forth, helpin' slaves out? I'll never know. You gotta do the same, girl. Push away any thought of Jake."

A long silence followed as they stared into the rain, thinking deeply about gone-away things.

"Been wonderin' why we're all chasin' after freedom." Liney's eyes glowed a warm brown. "Maybe freedom's just goin' ahead and not lookin' back. Us paddlin' on the rivers. Jake headin' his own way. Henry somewhere leadin' slaves on the underground."

Rain fell hard. Patches of ice floated past on the river. The runaways huddled in a circle to stay warm. Phoebe rested her head upon her friend's shoulder. The pine trees seemed to lean toward her like open arms. *This is the way things have to be. Rest. Forget. Fall into your dreams. Go on ahead.*

Phoebe shut her eyes, hoping for sleep, but all she saw was Jake's face. She remembered the morning in the shed and the one dark look between them before he ran. That look had been haunting her ever since. His eyes were full of secrets he could not tell her.

"Fly to freedom, girl," she imagined Jake telling her. "I couldn't stay with you. I had to run off so we could all go free."

Lots of folks been tellin' me what freedom is. All I know is something has to pass out of me first, all this achin'. Then freedom's gonna rush right in.

A wave of memories threatened to drown her. Phoebe thought she heard Jake finally whisper goodbye. She felt him loosen his hand from hers. Tears streamed down her face. *Something's passin' out of me. All this achin'.*

She slept on.

Late that night, something made Phoebe jerk awake. Bethy had rolled out of her arms and lay sprawled on the ground, barely breathing. Her lips shone like blue ice and her body felt stone-cold. Phoebe shook her hard but could not awaken her.

Liney awoke with a start and cried out, "Wake my child up!"

"Hush!" warned Phoebe. "She's frozen!"

They each lifted a stiff leg and a frozen hand, rubbing hard between their own cold hands to warm Bethy up. The child's eyelids fluttered open but she did not awaken.

"Bethy!" screamed Liney. "It's your momma. Wake up!"

Liney clutched her child and paced back and forth. Phoebe wrung her hands, not knowing what to do. *Here I've been worryin' about losin' Jake and right in front of my eyes, this little girl is driftin' away. I should have seen the signs. What would my momma do if this were her child?* She remembered how after picking cotton all day, her momma had greased down her blisters each night. *It wasn't just the medicine that healed me. It was my momma's touch. Healin' came right through her fingers.*

Phoebe opened her jacket and unbuttoned her shirt. "Give her to me."

She pressed Bethy to her bare chest and buttoned her shirt around her. At first, the child lay stiff against her but after a few minutes, Phoebe felt her own heat rise up like steam around the child. Little by little, the tips of Bethy's toes and fingers warmed. Then the shaking began. Bethy slammed her legs hard against Phoebe and screamed. She jerked so wildly that Phoebe had to hold her down to keep her inside her shirt.

"It's the thawing!" Liney worried. "Old Willie told me it hurts to have the blood rush back in."

A coughing fit broke up the child's cries. Phoebe rubbed Bethy's body up and down. She sang softly to soothe her.

And be-fo' I'd be a slave,
I'll be bu-ried in my grave.
Oh free-dom ov-er me!

Against her chest, Bethy finally stretched out and yawned. Phoebe nodded silently to Liney who sat straight up, squeezing Sarah. The older girl did not take her eyes off her little sister. She bit her lips so hard Phoebe knew she was trying not to cry.

But Liney couldn't hold back her own tears. "Why did I take my children?" she sobbed.

"We couldn't leave 'em behind," Phoebe reminded her. "They wouldn't be any safer on the plantation. Be sold away by now."

"If Bethy dies . . . it's all my fault."

Phoebe did not want to hear Liney talk like that. She

felt like shaking her friend. "You and me both decided we were strong enough to bring 'em out. We're gonna do it. Quit worryin'!"

For a few hours, Phoebe slept carefully on her side, with her arms folded around Bethy. She tried not to move. She did not let go. Rain fell in long sheets, soaking the ground beneath them. Endless rain like a mother's tears.

We have no medicine to cure this child. Gotta reach a safe station. We may have passed the first one by, but there's gotta be more. Old Willie and the steward both said that the Ohio is dotted up and down with stations. "Many friends will shelter you there." *The mapmaker promised, too.* Phoebe looked around the woods. Trees and more trees. No sign of any houses. *Please let us find a station*, she prayed. *I won't worry anymore if we do.*

When the rain stopped late that night, Phoebe carried Bethy gently while Liney dragged the raft back to the river. Sarah crawled aboard and they pushed off. The river had risen in two days, swelled with muddy water and swift currents the storm stirred up. Stiff wind blew Phoebe's cap off her head and flung her braids loose so that they flew wildly around and stung her cheeks. She paddled hard against the current. She pushed back with her field-tired muscles, dipping her paddle deep.

Phoebe no longer knew what she was looking for. She tried to think back to the steward's directions but no words came to mind. Dead ahead of them, a huge evergreen tree crashed down across the river. Their raft smashed flat against the tree trunk. Sarah clung to

Liney's neck and screamed. Phoebe lifted up Bethy, who was still sleeping, and tucked her inside her shirt again. She and Liney crawled off the raft onto the trunk. Liney reached out and yanked the raft over the trunk. The current splashed past them with a wild roar, drenching them all. Liney tried to hold the raft steady, but it was too slippery. It disappeared under the rushing waters and then bobbed up again. Finally she got a firm grasp on it and they all boarded it again.

Liney and Phoebe paddled stiffly. They could not stop shaking in their soaked clothes. Sarah huddled on Liney's lap to keep warm. Against Phoebe's chest, Bethy lay still. When Phoebe turned around to check on Liney, she thought she saw something slip along the western bank. She steered swiftly toward the opposite shore. Out of the woods stepped two dark figures. Sarah bolted to the far side of the raft, nearly tipping them over. The raft spun in circles. More shapes gathered by the water's edge on both sides.

They were surrounded.

A gun boomed by the bank of the swirling river.

"Stop or we'll shoot!"

Phoebe's paddle stopped in mid-air. Phoebe looked at Liney. There was a lost look in her friend's eyes. It echoed Phoebe's thoughts.

We have run so far. We have run so fast. We are trapped now!

"Steer that raft this way!"

Phoebe sat straight up. She guided the raft toward shore. Time froze. There was no sound. She had no thoughts. She felt only the wild pounding of her heart in her ears and her dreams sinking down into the swirling, brown waters of the Scioto River.

CHAPTER
TWENTY-FOUR

Patterson's Station

Phoebe stepped unevenly off the raft, with the dizziness of one who has sailed on water too long and forgotten the touch of solid ground beneath her feet. She pushed Bethy deeper inside her shirt and peered through the dark. As far as she could tell, about twenty men stood around them. More men came running out of the woods. All carried rifles strapped across their chests. Two men aimed their rifles straight at the slaves.

"This way!"

Phoebe felt the sharp spear of a rifle poking her back. It pressed through the layers of her clothes straight into her bare skin, urging her to move quickly. Liney stumbled beside her, clutching Sarah in her arms. Behind them, footsteps stamped heavily though the bush. The musky sweat odor of the white men filled the air. Phoebe suddenly could not breathe. She pulled in short gasps of air. Her thoughts raced. *Who are these men? Why are there so many of them stationed here? Are they slavecatchers or soldiers? Will they send us back South or keep us here? Please don't send us back! Please don't send us back!*

They marched a distance to a campfire in the woods. Phoebe stared at the man waiting there. By the light of the fire, his faded blue pants and jacket looked like a tattered uniform.

"At ease, men," he ordered. "Put down your guns."

"Captain, we pulled these three out of the river. Two men dragging a child. Maybe they're spies. Caught them sneaking by on a raft." The men gathered in front of the fire, and Phoebe now saw them clearly. They were dressed just like the man they had called "Captain."

"Who might you be?" the man in uniform demanded.

"Slaves from Alabama," Phoebe replied. Loosening her braids from her jacket, she nudged Liney to remove her cap. They both kept their eyes down. *Who were they? "Captain," the men called him.* She and Liney huddled with the girls around the campfire. Bethy gave no sign that she was awake.

"And why are you journeying on the Scioto?" the Captain kept on.

Something in his voice softened as he noticed Bethy's curly head sticking out of Phoebe's shirt. Phoebe raised her eyes. "We are lost, sir. We need your help."

"You are found," responded the Captain. He smiled at the slaves.

Phoebe's mouth dropped open. She stared straight at the Captain. Then she reached out for Liney's hand. *The password! Here in the middle of nowhere. We are safe!*

"Well, soldiers, looks like you caught women here, not men. They're runaways." He turned to Liney and Phoebe. "You've reached a Union camp, stationed near Circleville. Plenty of slaves pass through here on their way to Canada. It's December now. You have a month's long journey still ahead of you."

"Have we really come to a safe place, sir?" Phoebe begged.

The Captain glanced at his soldiers and hesitated.

"It's best for you to move on, but not just now." He looked toward the east, where the sky was brightening. "Slavecatchers can run into this camp, and I'd have to turn you over to them. It's the law. The only safe place is Canada."

"But, sir, someone's gotta help my child!" Liney clasped the Captain's hands in hers. "She's sick these past two days. Sleepin' deep. Not hearin' us. Cold through and through."

Phoebe lifted the child out of her shirt and handed her to her mother. The Captain peered at Bethy lying in Liney's arms, limp and pale. Then he looked at Sarah, skinny as a dried reed, who was watching him silently.

"It's nearly dawn. Rest here. Tonight, go to Patterson's Station, about four hours north. He'll know what to do." The Captain paused. "When you see the town of Columbus all lit up, stop. It's surrounded by slave-catchers. Too many stations have been discovered. Get out of the Scioto. Rip that raft apart. Leave no trace behind. Then walk northeast to Patterson's Station. First cluster of houses you come to is where it stands."

"But how will we know which house it is?" asked Liney.

"In Ohio, stations burn a candle in an upstairs window. But they've been using that signal so long that they're afraid slavecatchers may know of it. All the stations along the Scioto have been warned not to light their candles. Instead, look for a chimney with a line of white bricks painted on. That's another sign."

No wonder we couldn't find anywhere to stay, thought Phoebe. *No candle to show us the way.*

"In the meantime, you should rest and eat. Got that stew ready yet, men?"

The slaves soon warmed themselves by the campfire. Their clothes began to dry. The soldiers left steaming cups of stew and tea for them. Liney sat Bethy up but the child would not eat. She hung her head listlessly. Liney forced hot tea down the child's throat. Bethy was soon fast asleep on her mother's lap. Phoebe's eyes felt heavy. It was an effort for her to take a full breath. Inside her chest was a knife-like pain. She wanted to close her eyes and be lifted up to the dreamplace again. Fly, light and free, to the North. But all her dreams had vanished when Jake left. Finally she slumped over and slept.

That night, they pushed off again. They paddled for hours, Bethy tucked inside Phoebe's shirt, next to her skin. She did not murmur or make a sound. *Let her cry, I don't care*, Phoebe thought. *At least I'd know she's still alive.* Phoebe kneeled, lifting her paddle without a splash. Arms that once pulled in cotton tightened against the water, pushing the miles behind her. She felt the rhythm of the water singing, the skim of the raft sailing over waves, and the slap of the cold north wind against her face. She did not stop one second.

Night run.

❖

A light shone ahead. Then another and another. Hundreds of lights marked the town of Columbus. Liney steered the raft to the east shore. When they stepped onto land, it was rock-hard with frost. They tore their raft apart and flung the pieces into the woods.

It was deep dark by the time they reached the first small village. Several houses huddled together by the woods, as if keeping warm against the cold winter's night. The runaways hid by the edge of the woods, frozen still. Behind one house, a large quilt, sewn of hay-yellow cloth, hung on a clothesline and flapped in the brisk wind. *Clap. Clap. Clap.* It waved to Phoebe. It glimmered like fool's gold in the moonlight, the only dot of color in all the brown December land. She felt drawn to the house. But clouds darkened the moon and it was too black to see high up to check for a chimney with a line of white bricks. Most of the windows were unlit. *Families are all asleep by now*, worried Phoebe. *We have come too late!* Phoebe pressed her hands against Bethy tucked in her shirt. She had little heat to give the child.

"Best we move on." Liney nudged Phoebe. "No sign here."

They turned away and started to walk back into the woods. Only Sarah looked around, her eyes suddenly bright in her long face.

"Look, Momma!" A candle suddenly lit up in an upstairs window.

Liney and Sarah linked hands and rushed back to the house. But Phoebe trailed behind, breathless. She held back the cough that threatened to push out.

"The quilt!" she panted when she joined them. "I knew it was a safe house."

"Looks so warm inside," Sarah echoed. "Must be the station."

They crept up to the house. Phoebe peered through the windowpane and tapped on it without thinking. One hard knuckle. One light. Three times. Liney bolted from the window, tugging Sarah to the woods. Phoebe froze. The next moment, a lantern shone in her face.

"Who may you be visiting us?"

Phoebe's heart leaped in her chest.

"You alone, miss?" A tall white man leaned out the door.

"Yes . . . no! I am lost."

Phoebe's heart pounded. The man looked down at her shirt where Bethy's head peeked out. Suddenly Phoebe did not care who he was. All she wanted was grab his hands and beg him to help. Someone had to save Bethy.

Then the man spoke. "Don't worry, miss. You and the child are found. Who sent you?"

"Union soldiers at Circleville sent us." Phoebe glanced back into the woods.

"Go get your friends. You reached Patterson's station."

As Phoebe hurried to lead Liney and Sarah inside, she glanced up at the roof. The windows in the house were bright with light now and up above on the roof, she thought she could see a chimney with a line of white bricks.

Mr. Patterson smiled at them. "It's as if you were waiting for me. I just lit that candle now. Been waiting for a late hour, so no slavecatchers see it."

"Sarah saw it just in time. Something about that quilt, too," exclaimed Phoebe. "Flapping in the breeze so free as if it were calling me."

"We just changed the signal the other day. Conductors in Ohio decided to hang a quilt out to confuse slavecatchers. We have to protect runaways — and ourselves."

As the man spoke, Phoebe unraveled Bethy from her shirt and laid her flat on the table. The child looked as tiny as a doll. She seemed to have grown smaller on the trip. Wrinkles lined her forehead like an old person's face.

"Traveling a long while I see." Mr. Patterson's glance strayed to Bethy.

He bent over her, listening with his ear to her chest, a hand over her lungs, counting out her breaths as if he were a doctor.

"Short breaths. Wheezes. Sleeping deep," he noticed. "How long has she been this way?"

"Two, three days. Mighty quiet this past week."

"Any coughing?"

"Yes," remembered Phoebe, "'til she gave out."

Sarah stared back and forth from the stranger to Phoebe. Tears streamed down her face. "What . . . what's the matter with my sister?" she sobbed.

Liney reached out and held her oldest daughter.

"Sleeping in the damp too long," Mr. Patterson said as he hurried over to the fireplace. "This child's got lung fever."

"Is she . . . gonna get better?" Liney asked anxiously.

Patterson quickly set a pot of water to boil, sprinkling pine needles into it. He fanned the steam over Bethy's face.

"I've seen slaves come and go with lung fever. Young and old. Runaways all," he said, covering Bethy with a feather comforter. "But it looks like you got here just in time. She'll get rest and healing herbs now."

The three of them watched as he brewed purple flowers in hot water and eased a few drops of tea down Bethy's throat.

"Coneflower," he explained. "Old Indian remedy. If she can sweat it out, she'll pull through."

"What can we do, sir?" Liney wrung her hands.

"Keep watch. Boil water. Stay hid. You'll be safe here." The conductor led them to a back room where there were a couple of beds, covered with white sheets. He set down food and cider and the coneflower tea. He was just about to leave when Phoebe began to cough. Hard, barking coughs from deep in her chest. She could not speak for minutes afterward.

"You must be careful, miss, or you will end up sick, like this child," the conductor said in concern. He paused in the doorway. "Sip some of the tea. You need it."

But Phoebe was only thinking of Bethy. When the conductor left, she laid Bethy on one of the beds and held her hand. Beside her, she heard Sarah sobbing and reached out for her hand, too. She remembered praying in the swamp. That's when she needed prayers the most. She also remembered praying back home, too, that someone come tell her where freedom was and now she was more than halfway there.

Prayin' makes things happen, she decided. *I've forgotten to do it. Closer we get to promised land, the more I should pray.* She sat still for a long while. The cold December night, Sarah's cries, even Liney's worried face faded away. When she opened her eyes afterward, her body felt lighter, as if she'd been off flying somewhere. By her side, Sarah looked up, waiting for her to speak.

"I thought we were finished on the river." Phoebe smiled and set her arm on Liney's shoulder. "But it's all turned around. Prayin' helps."

"Prayin'!" Liney stepped back. "I sure didn't pray for this trouble."

"I prayed by the evergreens that we'd come to a healin' place," Phoebe said softly. "Patterson says we got here in time."

But Liney wasn't listening. "All my fault. Old Willie warned me not to take her."

Liney's eyes were fixed on Bethy. All this time the child had not moved. She placed one hand on her child's forehead. It was hot and dry.

Phoebe spoke up, "Liney, I got a feeling."

"What now, girl?"

"I know things. I knew I had to run from the planta-tion. I knew I'd follow Jake anywhere. I used to watch him Saturday nights, flyin' in those high jumps. I'd pretend I was right up there in the air with him, my belly flip floppin', my hand in his. Well, I got a good feeling now about Bethy . . . she's gonna be fine."

Phoebe hugged Sarah and she hugged her back. The young girl no longer cried. Phoebe pulled Liney to her, too, but her friend stood like a tree, hard and stiff. All that night, they took turns watching over the child, lifting her head to drink hot coneflower tea, waiting for the sign.

The next afternoon, in the dim light of a December day, Phoebe awoke first. Round beads of sweat sat on Bethy's forehead. A red flush glowed on her face. When Mr. Patterson stepped in soon afterward with dinner, he found them all gathered around Bethy.

"Mr. Patterson! Look!" Phoebe called.

The conductor placed a cool hand on the child's forehead and listened intently to her heartbeat.

"It's breaking loose. Boil up more pine needles. Quickly!"

The women rubbed pine needles into a pot and fanned the woodsy smoke over the child's face. Mr. Patterson patted Bethy's back until she coughed loudly. Her breath flew back, deep and strong, and her eyes popped open. She reached out for her mother.

Liney squeezed her hand. "Child, I've been worried sick about you!"

"Momma, is this freedom? Nice and warm here."

Liney gathered her in her arms and rocked her back and forth, tears streaming down her face.

"My baby," she whispered, "you've come back to me."

"Mr. Patterson must have heard all your prayers, Phoebe," Liney said as she laid Bethy back down and looked up at the conductor. "Thank you, kind sir."

"When healing comes, we can all thank God," Mr. Patterson replied, nodding his head. "You'll soon be on your journey again. But first you need to rest and get your strength back."

Mr. Patterson disappeared, then returned with a steaming cup of coneflower tea for Phoebe. She sipped it with her eyes closed, the steam billowing into her face, relaxing her.

Meanwhile, Sarah had crawled so close to Bethy, she was almost sprawled on top of her, wrapping herself in the comforter, too.

"Bethy!" she cried. "Where have you been?"

Bethy sighed. "Been dreamin' I was lyin' in a soft white bed."

"You are lyin' in a soft white bed," Sarah pointed out.

"I am?" Bethy looked down and gasped. "Where am I?"

"Closer to Canada," said Liney. "Closer to freedom."

Sarah tugged one of Bethy's cornrows. "You gotta get better real soon. We got lots of games to play on the way to Canada."

When Bethy fell asleep that night after sipping hot broth, Liney sat back on her heels and looked at Phoebe. She smiled for the first time in weeks, a sad, tired smile that stretched across her lean face.

"We sure are different, girl."

"What do you mean, Liney?"

"You lived with your family on the same plantation you were born on. Even though you lost your sisters and Isaac to the auction block, folks you loved were around. Your parents. Rachel. Old Willie. Emmett. You had time for dreamin' and lovin' both. That's the way it's supposed to be."

"How was your life different?"

"I got darkness wrapped all 'round mine. Started with that red cloth in Africa. Bad luck ran through my family. Bought my momma up when I was four. Overseer killed my daddy for runnin' after her. Just when I thought I'd have someone, Henry left. I had nothin' but darkness. Only rays of light have been these two girls. I never should have brought 'em on the underground."

"It wasn't any safer to leave 'em behind in slavery."

"Been heavy on mind this whole trip, worryin' about 'em."

To be a mother is to worry, Phoebe realized. *Sounds like something my momma would do. Bet she's sittin' up worryin' plenty, wonderin' where I am. Will she ever forgive me?*

"Bethy and Sarah gonna find freedom along with us," Phoebe reminded her friend. "No one's gonna get a chance to hurt 'em. When they're grown, they won't remember the South."

"You're right, girl. My young ones gotta have better than us. But I sure wish they'd turn out more like you when they grow up."

"When I first met you, Liney, I wanted to be just like you. Strong and smart. Full of mystery. Secrets couldn't tell me."

Stories. Sorrows. It's how we know one another. Now I know your secrets, Liney, and you know mine.

The two women hugged. Liney's body against Phoebe's was softer now, giving, like spring earth.

Liney laughed, "See how we're different? I'm the one who worries for us all."

"What about me, Liney?"

"You're the one who believes for us all." Tears shone brightly in Liney's eyes.

That night, everyone slept deeply.

CHAPTER TWENTY-FIVE

Alum Creek

Two days later they prepared to go. "Run now. The child is healed." Patterson pointed east. "Alum Creek lies in back of the swamp over there. It's a Quaker town. A two nights' walk. Find Benedict's house. He'll lead you to Sandusky. Remember the signals and you'll be sure to find him."

Even Sarah had memorized them, repeating them to the conductor. "May be a candle burning in an upstairs window. If there isn't, look for a ring of white bricks on a red chimney. Quilt on the line, too."

Mr. Patterson smiled at the child as he handed over four woolen blankets. "Keep those girls and you nice and warm," he said to Liney. "Carry them around your shoulders like coats."

Phoebe ran east over the frosted ground, past darkened houses, through woods that wrapped around them with giant evergreens, past the lone cry of a wolf. She flew straight across the cold gray land like a dark shadow flitting by. Running was the only thing that warmed her. Stopping for even a few minutes, she felt the numbing cold creep in again. But if she ran too fast, her chest ached and she lost her breath. She ignored the cough that choked her each morning. And the piercing pain that settled in her lungs, growing sharper with each breath. *Best to keep runnin'*, she thought.

Sarah grasped Phoebe's hand. "I'm runnin', too." The child skipped beside Phoebe, until her feet could no longer step, until they skimmed the ground, until she was set high upon Phoebe's shoulders. She spent the night there, ducking tree branches, watching stars in the black sky dip down to touch the earth. She seemed to be forever watching.

Liney stumbled behind, hugging Bethy to her, so far behind that the two women could not talk or signal one another. Phoebe worried that her friend walked slower as they neared Alum Creek.

We never needed words before to know what each of us was thinkin'. Liney was never slow before. It was her who taught me to be quick, whatever I do. She did not ask why Liney strayed behind, dragging her sore leg, instead of flying like a night bird across the north toward freedom.

They rested under gray December skies the next morning. Dampness settled deep in their bones. They wrapped themselves deep inside their woolen blankets and slept.

Finally the dream returned. Phoebe floated above the stone-cold earth like a cloud. Her white dress blew all around her and carried her high above the earth like wings. The North Star drilled a bright light through the sky. She flew toward it like a moth. All the cold in her melted.

> *If I just had two wings,*
> *bright an-gels a-bove,*
> *I would fly a-way to the king-dom,*
> *bright an-gels a-bove!*

That afternoon when Phoebe awoke with her head on the bare brown earth, snow flurries spun in a million directions. Snowflakes fell onto her face. She had never seen snow before. It was so bright. *The dreamplace is comin' closer to us!* She stretched herself awake. Her body felt strangely light and free, full of dreams to keep her running.

As if something's passin' out of me, something hard to give up. All this aching. Let it pass.

She remembered the dream that lifted her up from the plantation and carried her far away, the dream she thought she had lost with Jake. The last time she spoke of it was when they had danced in the attic at Ripley Station. *If we ever reach a safe place*, she had promised herself, *I'll come close to you.* Phoebe lifted her arms and spun in circles with her face held up to the sky. The white dress slipped over her like a cloud. Jake's honey-brown eyes seemed to watch her. A pressure swelled in her chest and her throat ached like she was going to cry. She spun and spun until the words stopped her.

"Girl!" Liney's voice was stern. "What are you doing?"

Three pairs of brown eyes watched her from the ground. Liney and the girls crouched inside their blankets, frozen still.

"I feel so free." Phoebe reached down and lifted Bethy up. "Let's dance! I wish I could fly all the way there."

Sarah soon begged for her turn to be lifted up by Phoebe and spun in circles high in the clouds of white snow. The girls chirped like birds in her arms, forgetting the worn shoes on their feet and the deep-down dampness that penetrated through all the layers of clothes they wore. They felt only the heat that came from Phoebe.

Summer heat.

Liney did not move. She watched them from her blanket with a gray film over her eyes. A single tear fell down her cheek and froze.

Late that night, they walked on. The rhythm of freedom sang in Phoebe and she could hear nothing else. With each step, she pushed the South farther behind to a place where she could no longer remember it.

Hours later, they passed a village. From the woods, they could see a sign announcing its name, but they could not read it. All the houses were dark. Liney stared closely at each house. No signals here. They kept walking. *We have walked two nights like Patterson told us but we haven't found it yet. Maybe we have come too far east*, wondered Phoebe.

Phoebe turned around, startling Liney, dragging her feet, dreamlike, yards behind her. She motioned Liney to follow her northwest. Another hour passed by. The cold, wet snow penetrated her shoes, then her socks. She stumbled on. Finally, at daybreak, they saw another town. Behind her, Phoebe heard Liney's footsteps stop. She spun around. Her friend pointed to a house. A ring of white bricks circled its chimney. They rushed over to it. Phoebe knocked the double knock on the heavy oak door. Three times.

A thin white woman dressed in black opened the door. She peered outside with a frown, lifting a lantern high.

"I knew it would come to this. What shall I do?" Her eyes darkened with worry when she saw them.

"Ma'am." Liney paused in the doorway. "Is this the house of Benedict at Alum Creek? We are lost souls come to find him."

The woman's hands flew to her heart. "My husband, Benedict, was arrested this night for hiding a family of slaves from Alabama. They are all in jail right now!" She pulled them inside, snuffing out her lamp. "They can hang him for it. They'll do the same to us. You can't stay here! How I wish I could lead you farther. Only my husband knew the way."

"Let's get out of here!" Liney edged toward the door.

"Wait!" The woman stopped Liney and the others. "You can't stay outdoors. It's below freezing. There's a barn at the end of this road, on a dead-end lane, where Old Tobias keeps his animals. It's almost morning. The law will soon begin its patrol. You must hide or ru —"

Phoebe's sudden coughing spell interrupted her. Phoebe leaned against the wall, holding herself up, suddenly breathless. She wanted to ask about the family from Alabama but the words had choked in her throat.

Was Rachel with them? Has she been captured, too?

"How long have you been running, young lady?"

"'Three months."

"Mainly on the rivers?"

Phoebe nodded.

"That's too long. That cough doesn't sound good. I'll brew some coneflower tea. You should stop and rest, but you have to reach the border before the year's end or you'll never make it across to Canada. It's too risky to cross over the lake come deep winter. The cold will likely freeze you all to death. Follow me."

The conductor's wife led them into her kitchen, motioning them to sit. She busied herself boiling water and gathering biscuits, cheese, and apples for their backpacks. Although they were inside a warm house, Phoebe shuddered through and through, suddenly chilled, as if she still wandered in the woods somewhere. The woman gave her a steaming cup of tea. *Lung fever!* Phoebe guessed with a shiver. She sipped the bitter brew and shut her eyes.

Don't know if I'm ever gonna see the other side. Don't know if it's real sometimes. So tired. If I could just get there and rest awhile in some soft white bed 'til winter's over. Why do I want to rest so bad? Never wanted to before. Why can't I stand up straight?

"You alright, girl?" whispered Liney, like a mother, close by. Bethy and Sarah stared at her with huge eyes.

"'Course I am."

"I can't bear to think of anything happenin' to you. You been so strong, so sure, pushin' us ahead."

"Quit worryin' about me, Liney!"

"I'll quit worryin' when you get better, girl! I'm just about worn out, through and through."

Phoebe gulped down all her tea and turned to Mrs. Benedict. "Tell me about that family, please! I am searchin' for my sister. Can't go on until I find out what's happened to her."

"Well, they had such troubles getting this far. Five of them had joined up. But somewhere along the Scioto, they got chased by slavecatchers. The boy was shot. No one knew if he was captured or dead. The rest ran here, carrying the girl. They stayed on too long, I suppose."

Phoebe pleaded, "What was wrong with the girl?"

"She was shot in the shoulder. My husband insisted she stay until she healed. But that girl was mighty restless. I remember her showing me her necklace. 'It's the color of my grandpa's dreams,' she said. 'I have to get there.' But she disappeared the night before the arrest."

All the blood seemed to drain out of Phoebe's face. *Rachel!*

In the dark kitchen, Liney squeezed Phoebe's hand. "You mean that girl wasn't captured with the rest?"

The woman shook her head. "Not with them, no. All she talked about was that boy. She went back for him, I suppose. She risked her life doing that. But she saved herself from capture here."

Wagon wheels pounded along the road. Liney jumped to her feet. The woman rushed to a window and looked out. The wagon rolled on.

Mrs. Benedict handed them the food. "Quickly now,

run to the barn. Don't come back here, whatever you do."

Outside, the stars had dimmed. It was almost morning. The hand of frost had turned everything white. They raced down the lane into the barn. A warm current of air drifted to their noses with the sharp odor of manure. Straw rustled. Animals shifted against one another. A sleek black horse snorted at them. They crawled into the stall with it and Liney and the girls quickly went to sleep.

A heavy weight seemed to press down upon Phoebe's chest all that morning. She tried to sit up to cough but could not. All through her journey, she had hoped to catch up with Rachel or to hear good news about her. But Mrs. Benedict's words had just made her worry more. Finally she, too, fell asleep.

Liney was awake and already sitting up when Phoebe opened her eyes that afternoon. "We're hidin' in a dead-end road for a reason." Liney's voice scratched in her ears as thin and dry as parchment paper.

"Why is that, Liney?" Phoebe lay deep down in the straw with the girls curled up flat against her, trying to keep warm.

"'Cause we have reached a dead end ourselves. Benedict knew the way to Canada. No one else. There's nowhere to go if he doesn't get free. May as well be in jail with those poor souls from Alabama."

Mr. Patterson led us to the Quakers at Alum Creek and never told us what to do next. Our instructions end here. Phoebe felt herself beginning to panic and tried to push her feelings down.

"Must be somebody who knows the way," argued Phoebe. "Must be a map somewhere to show folks where Canada is."

"No one's gonna show slaves a map to Canada!" snapped Liney. "If they did, we can't read it. Besides, it don't tell which road is safe. Someone's gotta tell us the way or we may as well go back."

Phoebe glanced down at the sleeping children and covered them with the blankets and more straw. "You're driftin' farther away from me each day," she sighed. "Worryin' all the time. What's botherin' you?"

"I got a lot on my mind, girl." Liney did not look at her.

"I thought we were done with secrets. You told me all about Henry. We're like sisters, Liney."

"Something's brewin' inside my mind like a pot of tea. Makin' me edgy. Wearin' me out. You're leadin' us on now. I'm just keepin' an eye out for trouble. We sure are in plenty of it now."

"We've been in trouble lots of times and it worked out," Phoebe pointed out. "Remember when we were in the swamp and couldn't find a way out and later when the Union soldiers caught us? Just when we thought we were finished, it was like startin' up again."

"Well, this sure smells like a dead end to me." Liney folded her arms across her chest. "A cold one, too!"

Phoebe saw a distant place in her friend's face that her words could not touch.

All that day they were alone in the barn. There was little to do and too much time to think. Perhaps the law was patrolling as Benedict's wife warned. They had eaten all the food from the backpack earlier. Now, they broke ice in the water trough and drank water alongside the horses. Phoebe choked on the cold water and coughed so deeply it hurt her chest. Pressing her hands over her mouth, she hid her head in the straw and spat up blood. It stained the straw bright red.

Then the shivers began. At first, icy chills ran up and down her spine, followed by flashes of summer heat. She felt herself sinking down and down, deeper in the straw, down into sleep.

Dreamshapes flew across her mind. She seemed to be following a trail of footprints by the Scioto River. For a moment, Phoebe caught a glimpse of Rachel's long braids flying behind her. When she looked up, she saw Jake running from the slavecatchers and disappearing in the rows of sea-island cotton. She ran all the miles back South to find him, but found herself home instead. Echoes of the past whispered in the slave cabin like dust. Her mother was silent and her father's back was turned away. Something floated high above her. It was the white cotton dress. She reached up but could not grasp it. She felt herself falling, sinking down onto the dirt of the cotton fields. For days she lay, thirsty and alone. The sun shone blazing hot. When at last she looked up, an ebony-skinned man stood straight as a scarecrow before her, pointing North. She rose up and ran across the frozen land always ahead of her, ran until she could run no more, stretching her arms out wide.

Then clouds of deep white snow buried everything. She covered herself in all that whiteness and slept.

CHAPTER TWENTY-SIX

Freedom Has a Color

Late that afternoon, they awoke to yelling. They swept more straw on top of themselves and burrowed deeper.

"I said I'd take you by his barn and here it is. Tobias is laid up with arthritis and can't take you himself," shouted a deep male voice that Phoebe thought too loud.

"Well, Mr. Goodman, let's have a look inside," another man ordered. "We'll see if Tobias can lend us a good horse."

The barn door creaked open. The black horse swung its head around and neighed loudly at the men. It stamped its foot down, grazing Phoebe's back. She did not flinch.

"Let's grab these horses. We got to bring those runaway slaves back South today. Collect a big reward if we do."

"These animals are all Tobias owns," argued Goodman. "Why don't you go to town and buy some horses?"

"That black horse looks like he's been storing winter fat and needs a good run. Let's look him over."

"Stop!" Goodman shouted. "This is all the poor man has. Leave him be. There are others you can make a deal with."

"Let's ride into town and see if you're right, Goodman. If no one is willing to sell their horses, we'll head back for this one." The barn door slammed so hard, it shook Phoebe's body.

An hour later, the runaways still hid deep in the straw, not daring to move. Phoebe's thoughts whirled in her head like a thunderstorm. *We can't leave the barn in daylight*, she thought. *We are trapped*. She had no strength to get up. All she craved was sleep and warmth. The pounding of horse's feet outside startled them all.

"Whoa!"

Wagon wheels screeched. Heavy footsteps. The barn door swung open. A knuckle rapped against wood. One heavy knock followed by a light one. Three times.

"Ladies, I know you're in there," announced the man in his loud voice, his words full of urgency. "Come out now."

Silence. Phoebe listened. Liney listened. Sarah stiffened in the straw next to her mother. Bethy slowly opened her eyes.

"The law's coming back for the horses. I couldn't stop them. They'll be here soon. I have to take you out of here now."

Beside her, Phoebe felt Liney dig down deeper into the darkness of the straw. Phoebe nudged her but she did not move. Phoebe slowly lifted her head up through the straw. She felt dizzy. Everything looked blurry to her, although it was a clear, sunny day. Finally, the horse's hind legs came into view and then the man's brown eyes staring down at her.

"I see someone's got sense. We only have a few moments."

"Who are you?" Phoebe asked the man dressed all in black, holding a hat with a wide brim in his hands.

"John Goodman. A Quaker. Benedict's wife sent me here to help you. Crawl out of that straw and follow me."

He opened the door wide. In the bright light outside, Phoebe saw a wagon with its back flap up.

"Jump in quick!"

"Where you takin' us?" Liney unraveled herself from the straw.

"The only place you'll be safe."

"No place is safe for us slaves, sir," snapped Liney.

"Where I'm taking you is . . . to Sunrise by the lake!"

Everyone shot up as if a lightening bolt shot through them. *Sunrise!* The word came to Phoebe's mind and made her smile. She remembered the steward telling them that was the code word for Sandusky. When she had first heard that word, Phoebe pictured the sun rising in a new land across the lake. *Canada!* Phoebe braced her back against the stall and pushed herself to her feet. The room spun around. Her legs did not feel steady. She pressed her back firmly against the boards and watched Sarah and Bethy rush to the door, braids flying behind them. Ahead was the last station on the underground road. Freedom waited on the other side.

"Climb up!" He helped the girls into the wagon as Phoebe dragged herself over. Inside the wagon, rolls of coverlets were stacked with skeins of dyed yarn and boiled wool. "I weave wool coverlets in nearby Owl Creek come winter. The rest of the year, I ride as far east as New England and as far west as Ohio to sell them. I'll drop you at the Canadian border. Benedict had told me the way to the station there in case anything happened to him."

"How long will it take us?" Liney asked.

"Four days. It's December 19. You'll be across the border by Christmas if the weather holds. Let's go. The law will be here soon."

It was a long while before the two girls settled down. They rolled around in the wool, upside down and right side up. They tunneled beneath the coverlets and pounced on each other, giggling. Finally Liney hushed them.

Phoebe lay still and pale. She did not stir when Liney covered her with the woolen coverlets, which were red, white, and blue, the dyes bright from field flowers. The red blazed deep as blood. The blue was dark as ink. White ran through it all like clouds. Phoebe snuggled beneath the colors of their country, a country divided by north and south.

I did not know that freedom had a color but these are the colors, she thought. *Red, white, and blue. They are the colors of a country at war. A country that dreams of freedom. I am runnin', runnin' from my country. No comin' back.* The wagon wheels picked up the rhythm of her words. "No comin' back. No comin' back," they repeated as they bounced over the frost-roughened road.

We are headed for the border that divides my country and the next one like a sharp line between what is wrong and what is right. And I am runnin', runnin' from my country. No comin' back. No comin' back.

They rested in the wagon as it bounced over the frozen roads leading to Lake Erie. Phoebe's thoughts drifted like flakes of snow falling from all directions. She could no longer keep guard as she had all the long months of running. She was being carried across the country and she could finally rest.

There's a time for dreamin' and this is it.

She felt her body sink down between the coverlets as if hidden inside a cave. Suspended from night. Suspended from day. Thoughts rolled over her like endless waves, like dreams touching her, disappearing like vapors before she could grasp them.

When she shut her eyes, she saw the dreamplace, the hushed white snowlight of Canada. She had heard that folks in the North hoped for a white Christmas. A memory of a long-ago Christmas drifted back from a frozen place where she had hidden it. She saw a table set with pecan pie and roast pig. Her father and Isaac rested after the early morning hunt with the Master. Rachel chased Phoebe, filling the cabin with laughter. Hannah and Jenny came in, chores finished early. Her mother and Lucinda bustled about in their good dresses, faces flushed from cooking and carrying back the still-warm leftovers from the Williamses' kitchen. The memory pulled at Phoebe's empty stomach and then sunk deeper. Teardrops froze on her cold brown cheeks before they could trickle down her face.

My mother and father will sit down to say their prayers and eat without the million questions of Phoebe runnin' around the room. This Christmas will be silent like mine, with an edge of sadness around the day, of children missin', of Isaac, Lucinda, Jenny, and Hannah, sold long ago and never heard from, of Rachel, lost on the road. They will think of me, too, and wonder where I am, if I am safe, if I am one of the lucky ones who made it to freedom. My father will remember how his father's dream came to his two daughters and sorrow that they did not tell him.

It all spun in her mind like threads of cotton woven together. Memory and tears blurred her mind. *Will they forgive me? Will they believe someday that I did the right thing? How will they ever know what happens to me? Am I strong enough to make it?* She felt as if she were drowning in waves of sleep.

She awoke drenched in sweat. She lay flushed for a few minutes and then chills rocked her body until her teeth rattled hard. She coughed and spit up bright red blood.

"You alright, Phoebe?" Liney's voice sounded far away.

Phoebe remembered where she was, in the back of a wagon, headed to Canada. It was something real she could hold onto.

"You been sleepin' a long time," she heard Liney say. "Sleep on. Get your strength back. There's still runnin' to do on the other side." Liney drew a coverlet over her chest and tucked it around her. "Girls, lie next to Phoebe and warm her up."

Phoebe felt Bethy and Sarah snuggle up. She heard Liney's words whispering warm in her ear, her voice carrying a memory of home.

Sister. Brother. Mother. Father. Friend. Liney is all of them. Momma, Papa, you need not worry any longer. Liney is leadin' me. She thought I was leadin' us. But she's the one.

She slept on.

CHAPTER
TWENTY-SEVEN

Sunrise

Inside the wagon, it seemed like endless night. Phoebe lost track of the hours and the days. They slipped past her like moments. She drifted from one nap to another. From faraway, Sarah peered into her face. "You alright now, Phoebe?" Sometimes, she felt a light touch on her hand, like a small child's fingers tickling hers, then letting go.

At night, when they stopped to rest, Goodman built a campfire. He roasted lamb and sank potatoes deep in the coals to cook. Liney and the girls peered out of the wagon, wishing they could sit by the hot flames.

Goodman brought their dinner into the wagon and sat down to eat with them. "Someone may ride by at any time and catch us out there. Here, no one will see us. The food will help heat you up."

The Quaker brewed coneflower tea, too, as Benedict's wife had instructed him. He watched as Liney raised

Phoebe's head for sips of it. Phoebe listened to the two of them talking. They seemed far away although they sat beside her.

Goodman shook his head at Phoebe. "That girl looks worn out."

"She ran hard. Lost a friend on the road. Worryin' all the while about her sister, too." Liney told him how Rachel ran back to the Scioto, not yet healed from a gunshot wound, to find Samuel. Phoebe noticed how Liney spoke for her now. Liney seemed to have forgotten her own worries.

Tears poured down Phoebe's face. She did not have the strength to say one word.

Goodman sighed and patted Phoebe's hand. "Such sorrows you bear. When I go back, I'll stop at all the stations I know and tell them to be on the lookout for your sister. I know a conductor scouting the Scioto River. I'll write to him, too."

Phoebe smiled at him and fell asleep instantly. In her dreams that night, she saw two sets of footprints on the ground, side by side, as if two people held hands while they walked. *Help is comin'!* Phoebe called out to them.

◇

Finally, after four days of traveling, Phoebe's mind brightened shiny clear as starlight. Cold night air pressed through her coverlets. Phoebe awakened from the slumber that had crept over her body since she stopped at Benedict's. She stretched her legs out. Her feet were numb with cold and her chest ached whenever she took a deep breath. But her body no longer burned with fever.

The wind changed. It blew cold, Canadian air straight down from the north and dampness that could only come from water. They heard waves lap against the sandy shore and peered out. As far as they could see beneath the starlit sky, there was water in all directions. It spread wide like the ocean Phoebe imagined her ancestors once crossed. Around the water blinked dots of light here and there, houses shining in the dark. It was Lake Erie at last.

The wagon bounced along slowly in the darkness. A kerosene lamp swung back and forth beside John Goodman, throwing light and then shadow all around the wagon. Steady wind blew off the lake. Liney sat facing south, her eyes shining in the dark. The rest of them faced north. Phoebe rubbed Sarah and Bethy's hands and feet briskly to warm them.

"Make you ready for runnin'," she whispered.

Too soon the wagon stopped. Men's voices cut across the crisp cold air, border guards patrolling the port town of Sandusky.

"What may your business be this time of night?"

"I'm headed into town with a shipment of blankets."

"Good you're not passing over the lake. Storm's brewing on the other side. Nobody's out tonight. Move quickly, man."

"Aye. Goodnight."

Phoebe could have counted the steps of the horse's hooves as it trotted over the last mile. The wagon swayed back and forth. Time seemed to hang breathless in the black night, waiting. The girls sat straight up. At last, the wagon shuddered to a stop. Doors creaked behind them. Suddenly it was bright with light, windless, and warm. Goodman opened the flap and the stowaways slipped out.

In the lamplight, they saw the roof of a barn high above their heads. Goodman hurried to the door. He pressed his ear against a crack in the boards. Out of the shadows stepped a man with shiny copper skin and eyes black as coal. Phoebe gasped. The children gathered by Liney, listening still.

"Welcome to Dr. Tilden's barn," he nodded. "Lots of slaves stop here waitin' for the next safe boat to Canada."

"Who may you be, sir?" asked Phoebe, wide-eyed.

"Reynolds. Most folks think I'm just a slave with Cherokee blood runnin' through me, following my Master, the good doctor, around. But I'm a free slave, a conductor, leadin' slaves across with Dr. Tilden."

"All's quiet outside. Right cold," reported Goodman. "When do they cross?"

"Midnight tonight is when the *Mayflower* sails. I just led a slave onboard. He stayed for some weeks in this barn, waiting for his friends but they never came. I'll tell the captain that tonight four more slaves sail. The doctor will be back from his trip by then and travel with us." Reynolds slipped outside.

"Momma!" Sarah exclaimed. "A boat's gonna sail us to freedom!"

"We gonna be free?" asked her sister. "When?"

"Soon!" Phoebe promised. "Real soon."

That evening in the barn, they shared a last dinner with Goodman. Hot porridge from a tin pot. Crisp week-old bread. Steaming black English tea that heated them all the way through. It hit Phoebe's mind like a drug. For an hour, she paced the barn until her feet heated up and her heart beat fast. She shook her hands hard to warm them until they blurred the air.

"Quit that pacin', girl!" Liney's eyes narrowed. "Actin' like a wild animal in a cage. Makin' me nervous."

"We are so close! Wish I could fly there. Look what's about to come! Ridin' a boat across a lake. Travelin' by night to Canada. The other side just waitin'."

"Girl, you just got over being real sick. Shush now!" Liney looked pinched and worried again.

But Phoebe raised her arms high above her head and twirled. She felt the earth hum with the rhythm of freedom. Her dreamplace was close by. It made her want to sing and dance.

If I just had two wings,
bright an-gels a-bove,
I would fly a-way to the king-dom,
bright an-gels a-bove!

The girls rushed to her side and lifted their arms up to her.

"Remember that game we played up in the attic with you and Jake?" Sarah tugged hard on her sleeve.

Phoebe lifted Sarah up and spun her in circles around

and around. Sarah leaned her head back and stretched her arms out wide as if they were wings. She pretended she was flying through the air. Bethy cried for her turn next. Phoebe closed her eyes and imagined Jake spinning with them. She saw his fiery eyes, his leanness, and her, looking up at him. Tears streamed down her face. *How he would smile to reach promised land. How he wanted to take us there!* she remembered.

"Be still!" hissed Liney, her ear pressed to the door. "Someone's comin'!"

Reynolds slipped inside the barn, breathing hard. "I just walked past the *Mayflower*. Slavecatchers are pacing the docks. One carried a poster showing two female slaves with two young girls." He peered closely at their faces. "Looks just like the four of you."

Phoebe's heart raced. She and Liney stared at one another.

"It is us," Liney said. "They know we're runnin' together."

Reynolds hurried to the back of the barn and returned with new clothing. "These are disguises. You must appear like you've lived in the North for a while. And you must all be boys."

Liney immediately exchanged the girls' clothes for the dark jackets Reynolds gave her. She pulled their hair tightly beneath woolen hats, wrapped scarves to cover their faces, and helped them into boots. Phoebe snuggled into a navy pea coat, worn thin at the elbows and wrists. It was heavy and warm. She helped Liney into woolen overalls and a long black coat, trailing to her ankles.

Just as they were finishing, Dr. Tilden stepped into the barn. The doctor's hair was pure white like snow and his face shone bright. He set a traveling bag on the ground.

"We'll lead you to the *Mayflower*. Its Captain is a conductor. It's about to set sail soon. Walk behind me with your heads down, quiet as church mice, and pretend you are my slaves. Not one sound. Slavecatchers are all around us."

In the dim lamplight, Phoebe and Liney nodded their heads. They carefully tucked their braids beneath floppy tweed caps, pulling the brims low down, hiding their faces.

"Farewell!" said Goodman. "I'll think of you in freedom."

"Thank you, friend." Liney shook his hand. "We would never have found our way without you."

Phoebe put out her hand. "We'll always remember you bringin' us nearer to freedom. Please tell Mr. Benedict we pray for his release."

"I'll keep my word, Phoebe," Goodman promised. "If Rachel's on the road, we'll find her. I'll bring her to Sunrise myself. She'll meet you on the other side. Godspeed to you all."

Goodman rode his wagon out of the barn. Minutes passed. The night was quiet. The doctor pointed to a navy trunk with two straps.

"Carry this trunk between you. It's empty so it's light enough," he explained, picking up his own bag. "Make it look like we're traveling a long ways."

They stepped into the street. Here and there people passed by, bundled in winter coats, hurrying to the dock, their breath fogging the frosty night air. At the end of the street was the dock. In the moonlight, a huge ship waited there, painted red, deep as blood.

The *Mayflower*.

Liney stiffened beside Phoebe, drawing everyone to a halt. She stood like a statue, silent and still. Phoebe shivered. She felt something was about to crack open. She held her hands over her ears.

"Stop!" Liney ordered in a stone-cold voice.

No, Liney! We are almost there! If we don't walk straight onto this boat, something will happen. I just got enough strength in me to step aboard. We won't make it together if we stop now.

Dr. Tilden grabbed the trunk from their hands and pushed them into a nearby alleyway out of the glow of the gaslights.

"See here, woman!" demanded Dr. Tilden. "What's the matter?"

"I'm not boarding this boat!" Liney's eyes flashed wildly. "It's painted red. It's not safe! We gotta run out of this town."

Phoebe remembered Liney's story of the color red. "All that happened a long time ago," she urged. "Got nothin' to do with right now. Let's board before it sails. It's not safe to hang around."

Down the street, a foghorn blew twice. Ten minutes to board.

"I'm not goin'! That color is a curse. We won't ever

get to freedom if we board. Something's gonna go dead wrong."

Reynolds tugged on Liney's arm but she would not budge.

"Hurry, miss!" he begged.

Sarah looked up at her mother, as if wondering what the fuss was all about. She tugged Liney's hand and pointed to the steamboat.

"C'mon, Momma, I wanna go."

Bethy's bottom lip began to tremble. Soon, Phoebe knew, she would scream so loudly everyone would notice them.

"We can't go by water, child!" Liney's voice was tense. "We gotta stick to land."

What could go wrong? wondered Phoebe. *A full day's ride crossin' Lake Erie. We just have to pass the halfway line, the invisible line between this country and Canada where border guards patrol. If we make it past there, we'll be safe.*

"If you walk around this lake," warned Dr. Tilden with a grave face, "it'll take a month, maybe more in this weather. It'll be deep winter by then. Snowstorms every day. These young ones won't make it."

"We just ran clear across the country to get here, Liney," gasped Phoebe. "Been on the road four long months. All of us are tired. This kind man is bringin' us aboard. We're all goin' on."

She stared at her friend. Liney was all hard lines, bony, her face pinched thin. If only she could melt her. She reached out and touched her friend's hand. "The color red brought your family out of Africa once. Now it's gonna carry us out of slavery," she tried to calm her friend. "Must be a travelin' color. Not a trick color."

Phoebe held her breath and waited. Liney did not move. Phoebe remembered saying goodbye to Jake beneath the evergreens and how Liney had once helped her. And then she knew what had been troubling her friend all this time.

"Henry's pullin' you back, isn't he? He's stayin', but you gotta bring his children over. I saw him once in my dreams," Phoebe recalled. "When I felt like turnin' back, he stood tall in the cotton fields, ebony-skinned, pointin' the way north . . . to freedom."

Liney stood stiff and straight as she had once stood when Phoebe told her she was sold. Tears shone in her eyes but did not fall.

"He'd be proud of you for makin' it to Canada. Say goodbye to him. I'm boardin' now with the girls. Follow us."

Again the foghorn blew. Last call. Reynolds led Phoebe out of the alley. She reached out both hands for the girls, pulling them away from their mother, lifting Bethy onto her shoulders as she had done for most of the trip. *Let her come along behind us. Let her come!* She lifted one foot and then the other, stumbling across the frozen street. She felt a yank on her coat and knew it was Sarah trying to run back to Liney. Reynolds grabbed Sarah's hand and headed down the street. Bethy squirmed, trying to wiggle free, but Phoebe kept walking. Between them, Reynolds and Phoebe shared the weight of the trunk.

"Look proper now, children!" Phoebe demanded. "No cryin'."

The ache in Phoebe's chest was unbearable. She could hardly breathe. She heard no movement of footsteps behind her as she had hoped. Liney's decision had landed like an ax, opening up a deep pit of darkness between them all.

They reached the dock. Too late to turn around. Bystanders watched. Slavecatchers held posters in their hands, checking everyone's face as they passed by. Phoebe kept her head down. She felt their eyes drill right through her. A tall figure pacing the deck of the *Mayflower* suddenly halted, wrapped in a gray blanket from head to toe so Phoebe could not see their face.

"Hurry!" Dr. Tilden fussed loudly, pushing his way through the crowd. "You're my property and we've got a boat to catch!"

They stepped onto the gangway. A white man collecting money looked up when he saw them.

"Step up! Boat's sailing. How many boarding?"

Phoebe's heart pounded in her throat. She dared not turn around. She felt eyes watching them from the deck. She could not take one step farther. She was ready to break loose from Reynolds' arm and run down the street after her friend.

"Five —" Dr. Tilden paused, then announced. "No — six!"

Phoebe spun around. Liney stood behind them, shaking hard as a leaf left hanging on a winter tree. Sarah reached out for her mother's hand and they all drew

Liney to their side. Dr. Tilden pressed the passage money into the collector's palm.

"This way with the trunk," he ordered. "Down below."

At last they all boarded the *Mayflower*.

---◇---

CHAPTER
TWENTY-EIGHT

Above the Pine Trees

They had sailed all day. It was night again, always night. Liney paced the floor of the ship's cabin back and forth. Her worried eyes filled her face.

"I know they're out there. Sailin' in our trail."

"Who, Momma?" begged Sarah.

"No one's out there," Phoebe smoothed Sarah's hair. "Just night all 'round and miles and miles of water to cross over to freedom."

"No one's waitin'?"

"Sleep now. Gotta run once we reach shore."

Sarah snuggled next to Bethy and Phoebe rocked them to sleep.

Sometime that evening, the boat's engine stalled. An anchor splashed overboard. Voices called across the lake, border guards or slavecatchers. Reynolds looked up uneasily.

"Get in the trunk!" Dr. Tilden ordered them. "Hurry!"

The runaways squeezed inside. Bethy was half asleep, ready to pout. Sarah stroked her face, making her yawn. Above their heads, the lid slammed shut. A lock clicked. Darkness. Musty air. The boat swayed back and forth. Phoebe pressed against Liney and laid her ear over her heart. *Keep my mind on one thing so I won't hear anything else. Listen to my friend's heartbeat*, she thought. *Be invisible.* Ever so slowly in the darkness, she wrapped her arms around her three friends.

Thud. A boot landed on top the trunk. A chair creaked. Hands banged the lid. Above their heads, Dr. Tilden and Reynolds played a game of poker.

"How much do you bet on that hand?" the doctor said loudly.

Footsteps banged down the stairway. Questions. A heavy knock rapped on Dr. Tilden's cabin door.

"Why are we stopping, Captain?" yelled Dr. Tilden.

"United States border guards. They're coming in to have a word with you."

The door squeaked open. Boots pounded the floor. Phoebe felt Liney's shirt against her soaked with sweat.

"What are you checking, good men?" Dr. Tilden laughed. "Who's winning this poker game?"

"Where are you headed, sir?" the guard demanded.

"Point Pelee, Canada, to visit friends. Brought my best slave to attend me. I can't trust just any slave loose across the border. Most of them would run away. But this boy was born on the grounds of my mansion. Tried and true, he is."

"Where are your other slaves, sir?"

A pause. Liney's heartbeat drummed in Phoebe's ear.

"Safe and sound. Locked up tight. Back home."

"Then goodnight, sir, we were mistaken. Captain, we'll be on our way. This boat's clean. No runaways onboard."

The boat sailed on. Reynolds opened the lock on the trunk and was ready to lift the top when someone tapped on the door again. One hard knock. One soft one. Three times. Phoebe pressed her ear against the lid.

"Sir," someone begged. "I saw you board with some slaves. Two children. Two women. I've been searching for my family. One goes by the name of Phoebe. Is she with you?"

"Why, son, who may you be?" wondered Dr. Tilden.

"This is the slave who stayed with me, sir," said Reynolds. "He's —"

Phoebe did not wait for an answer but pushed hard on the lid of the trunk. She had this strange tingling, like something was busting loose inside of her. When she stepped out, her heart pounded in every cell of her body.

The man, both strange and familiar, stood before her, his gray blanket falling to the floor. He was leaner than she remembered and taller. He was all thinness. Even his clothes were thin from wearing them too long.

Jake!

"Girl, I've been waitin' on this day!" he cried out. "Almost gave up hope of ever seein' you again."

Phoebe opened her mouth but no sound came out, just a raw ache in the place where her words should be. She felt something run out of her — the dampness of dark places and the swirl of cold waters. She felt flushed with Alabama summer heat.

Remembering tears spilled onto her shirt.

"Phoebe, I got so much to tell you . . ."

Jake opened his arms in a full circle and Phoebe flew into them. She felt his body warm against hers as if it were just yesterday when they had danced in the attic. For long minutes all they heard was one another's heartbeat. Slow. Deep. Heavysweet.

Suddenly they were surrounded. Arms hugged them, widening the circle. Kisses. Tears. Dr. Tilden's laughter. A shout of joy from Liney. Bethy screaming to be picked up. Jake scooped her up and swung her high in the air until she beamed. Sarah tugged at Jake's sleeve, grinning, "Remember me?" Phoebe smiled at the wonder of Jake standing there. He had stepped out of a dim dreamspace into this cold December night.

"Where have you been, boy?" Liney teased. "This Phoebe's been worryin' about you as if we didn't have enough troubles!"

Jake set Bethy on the ground and watched Sarah chase her around the cabin. Then he faced his two friends with dark eyes. "Tricked those slavecatchers. Headed back to Ripley Station. I hid there, prayin' you rode safely off. I dreamt of fightin' but all I wanted was to be with Phoebe. Later I stopped by that shed I left you at. You were gone. I knew I had to go ahead."

Phoebe's mouth fell open. *Jake came back for me!*

"Waited in Tilden's barn for weeks. Reynolds ordered

me to sail tonight. Dragged my feet aboard. Then I heard Dr. Tilden fussin' and saw three of you and looked again. A fourth person trailed behind. I knew it was you."

"I thought these were your friends," Reynolds smiled. "I was waiting until we safely passed the halfway line to find you."

"Look over here, everyone!"

Dr. Tilden stood by the porthole. Phoebe ran over, pulling Jake with her. Stars dotted the sky with light. The small islands offshore Sandusky had disappeared. In the distance was a new shoreline dotted with pine woods.

Liney slipped beside her. The children rushed over too, tugging at their pant legs to be pulled up so that all five of them looked out the porthole together, hands pushed hard against the ship's side to see.

Sarah screeched in their ears, "Can-a-da!"

"The boat will reach Point Pelee before midnight and drop you off a distance before we land there," announced the doctor. "Tomorrow morning, you will reach Chatham."

"Midnight!" Phoebe spun around. "What day is this?"

"Christmas Eve. A fitting day for freedom," said Dr. Tilden.

The mapmaker told us we'd be in Canada by Christmas. All has gone well! All has gone well! rejoiced Phoebe.

Suddenly she felt Liney's arms wrap around her, good and strong.

"Phoebe, what is this feelin' come over me?" Liney's face shone full moon bright. "We have crossed over safe and something in me is changed. As if Henry's shinin' a light across this lake to freedom. All my worryin' has gone away!"

Phoebe grinned widely from ear to ear.

"That's the freedom feelin' Old Willie taught me about."

"All this time, I never understood why you were so sure. Lifted by dreams. Sometimes I wondered if your feet were on the ground."

Something old has gotta pass out first. Then freedom's gonna rush right in. Dreampower is runnin' strong through all of us now.

"You called us here," Jake whispered in Phoebe's ear. "We just followed you."

"It was Liney who pushed me out of the plantation." Phoebe's eyes sparkled. "You led us halfway, Jake. I just told everyone my dreams."

"Dreams were what we needed to hear," said Jake.

"You sure have changed, Phoebe," Liney admired. "Back home you hung your head down. Now you're lifted straight up. Pretty soon, you'll be taller than me!" Liney touched her hand to Phoebe's head, just an inch shorter.

Phoebe turned to Sarah. "Gotta get you girls ready. Can't go to Canada with your hair every which way. Promised land is what my grandpa called it. Goin' there is like steppin' into church."

Phoebe helped Sarah into her jacket and wrapped a blanket around her, before she sat the girl on her lap. She loosened her hair. It reached her waist, glossy black.

She braided it with shaking fingers, then tucked Bethy's cornrows in neatly.

At last it was full dark. Reynolds called them up to the deck. Point Pelee was so near, Phoebe thought she could reach out and touch it. In the moonlight, the ground gleamed white with snow.

The dreamplace. So bright and light it hurt her eyes.

"That's the way." Dr. Tilden pointed to a grove of trees by the light of the ship's lamp. "When you're out of the pine woods, head northeast. Storm's brewing. Keep walking. You'll get frostbite if you stop. By dawn, you'll reach Chatham. Christmas Day. Free slaves will shelter you there."

"That land's frozen solid." Reynolds shook his head sadly. "Wish there were a way to fly across it. Godspeed to you all!"

The boat stopped by the shoreline. Jake jumped ashore first. The two women followed, holding the children in their arms. For just a few steps they walked and then they ran together as if they had never stopped. Before the *Mayflower* sailed off, they were headed in the direction of the pine trees.

For long hours they ran across the frozen woods, panting in gasps that pulled hard on their lungs. They did not stop to catch their breath. Sweat cooled into ice on their backs. Frost cut into their bare ears and fingertips. Crystals sparkled in the air like specks of frozen light. Snow swirled in a million directions. North, south, east, and west it spun, all around them. It snowed so heavily in front of them, they could no longer see where they were going.

Beyond the pine trees must be the way. I have to reach it! No Master, no slavecatcher can stop me now. Phoebe dragged her frozen feet like lead. She pulled Bethy along until she could pull no more, then she lifted her high upon her shoulders and entwined her arms around her. Phoebe's breath made streams of fog that spread out from her body like clouds. She heard the crunching of her feet over snow, her body heavy beneath the weight of carrying Bethy. She looked up at the sky. Almost dawn. She passed Jake by.

Liney slowed down.

"I don't rightly know how to go across this free land."

"Just keep runnin'!" exclaimed Sarah.

All this time as she had been carried in Liney's arms, she had not spoken. She looked straight ahead to the pine trees.

Liney stopped. "Let's watch Phoebe to see what she does." She yanked Jake to slow him down, too. "This is the land she's prayed for. Let Phoebe go ahead. Freedom's gonna find her first. We'll be right behind watchin' it come upon us."

Behind them, they heard the gong of the border guard bell tolling from the lake. *Christ-mas morn-ing!*

Liney reached out her strong brown arms, arms that had once pulled in cotton beside her and pushed Phoebe.

"Fly, girl!" Liney pointed dead ahead. "Fly to freedom!"

Phoebe's feet stepped lightly now. She no longer felt the burden of the child clinging to her neck. She stepped again and her feet did not touch the ground but touched clouds of snow instead. She raised her arms up to the sky and felt herself lifting up, flying across the white land high above the pines. Her white cotton dress swept through the sky like wings.

All her life she would remember coming into the white land, touched by clouds of snow that flew from every direction until she shone bright as snowlight. Her brownness was covered in light. Her face was brushed by crystals from heaven. Bethy was blanketed in snow. Far below, Sarah, Liney, and Jake looked up at them.

Her sorrows seemed light as feathers. Her stories spun away.

She would remember flying until she landed in the white land and was covered with all that whiteness. The lights of Chatham shone in front of her. The dream-place. Church bells chimed. *Christ-mas morn-ing! Christ-mas morn-ing!* It was dawn. *Sunrise!* Free slaves stood in the streets ahead watching her land. They rushed toward her with their arms wide open to lift her and the child. Fathers. Mothers. Sons. Daughters. They welcomed them home.

Phoebe and Bethy were held by hundreds of hands the color of the earth. Indian brown. Coal black. Molasses. Hemp. Phoebe collapsed in their arms. Jake and Liney rushed to her side with Sarah.

Phoebe remembered the song she had heard only once before, when Old Willie first got his wings. Memory voices rose up like a flame somewhere singing brightly. The words shivered through her, raising goose bumps up and down her body.

She opened her mouth wide. She shouted so every single slave could hear — slaves still toiling in the cotton fields and runaways on the underground road.

Toll de bell, An-gel, I just got o-vuh!
Toll de bell, An-gel, I just got o-vuh!
I just got o-vuh at last!

Somewhere faraway, slaves lifted up their heads to listen. Lucinda at her washtub. Jenny with her newborn in her arms. Hannah walking to the cotton fields. Isaac awakening in the dark. Rachel dreaming inside a safe house in Ohio with Samuel watching over her. They all paused. They felt the words brush against them, like a light breeze, reminding them of their dreams. Henry, too, stopped on a trail, a family of slaves behind him, and looked north. On the plantation, her momma and papa rolled over in their sleep, softly dreaming, the cornhusk doll forever between them.

Reborn song. Joyful sound.

---◇---

AFTERWORD

They touched their brown feet to the earth and ran.
The earth shook.
Time shifted.
A river rushed. Thunder rolled.
There was enough time for a black shadow
to slip between earth and sky.
Another shadow followed. And another.
The earth shook with the rhythm of slave's feet
running north.
Slipping between borders at dusk.
Riding the Ohio nighttimes.
Searching for a red chimney with a line of white bricks,
a quilt flapping on the line
and a single candle burning upstairs.
Filling the earth with the shining white light of freedom.
Whitelight. Homelight. Freedomlight.
Singing the names of friends in freedom.
    Phoebe. Jake. Liney.
    Sarah. Bethy.
    Gone to freedom.
                            Amen.

---◇---

AUTHOR'S NOTE

This book began with Phoebe. One night, as I was doing research on slavery, her face appeared in my mind. She looked tortured, thin, on the run. She had something she yearned to tell me. As I listened to her story, I longed to help her. Then I remembered reading a folktale in which Africans once had the power to fly. They lost this magic when they were chained down and shipped as slaves to America. Phoebe would be the one, I felt, who would remember the ancient power of her ancestors. How would she discover this ability? Through dreams. Dreams give us access to the past and sometimes, the keys to unlock our problems. Dreams help us to imagine new lives and also to survive in intolerable situations. Phoebe had to dream or lose hope. By doing so, she not only reclaimed her African heritage but also found freedom.

I gathered authentic stories of the African slave trade

from: B.A. Botkins' *Lay My Burden Down* (University of Chicago Press, 1933) and Julius Lester's *To Be A Slave* (Dial/Scholastic, 1968), books that developed from the Federal Writers' Project in the 1930s, based on actual slave interviews. The central image of flying originated from the folktale, "The People Could Fly", as told by Virginia Hamilton in *The People Could Fly* (Knopf, 1985), a study documenting the slaves' strong belief in a spiritual deliverance out of bondage.

Slaves could not really fly, but their faith and desire for freedom must have been like wings that helped to carry them as they took a risky journey on the Underground Railroad (UGRR). The UGRR has always fascinated me. Secrecy. Danger. Escape. I discovered that although stations existed in the South, they were scarce, less organized as a system, and subject to such strict secrecy that information about them was often never recorded. However, the northern UGRR system was in existence for over a century and, although conducted in secrecy, was documented by famous conductors such as William Still, Levi Coffin, the Reverend Mitchell, R. Smedley, and Eber Pettit, as well as numerous local station keepers. Wilbur Siebert's books, *The Underground Railroad from Slavery to Freedom* and *Mysteries of Ohio's Underground* became my primary sources as I researched at the Shomberg Center for Research in Black Culture and the Central Library of the Queens Borough Public Library.

I included actual stations and names of conductors in Ohio, the most well-traveled state on the UGRR route.

One station, the Rankins' house in Ripley, sheltered more than two thousand runaway slaves who passed by. The following are historically documented: Rankins at Ripley Station; Union Camp at Circleville; Patterson's Station; Mr. Benedict at Alum Creek; John Goodman as a weaver; Reynolds as an agent at Dr. Tilden's barn in Sandusky (i.e., "Sunrise"); the *Mayflower*, an abolitionist boat to Pt. Pelee, Canada; and the community of fugitive slaves that settled in Chatham, Ontario. Similarly, the UGRR passage across the Kentucky, Scioto, and Ohio rivers by raft and steamboat, trails through the Smoky Mountains, use of passwords and code words, the help of Quakers, the river signals, marks of a "safe house," "lung fever" in runaways, use of the Native American herb, coneflower, for healing, "gentlemen's agreement" or promise between the North and South during the war to return runaways to plantations, plantation patrols, and the secret use of hideaways to shelter slaves.

I have emphasized the role of traditional song in Afro-American culture. Songs were often the only outlet and expression of this oppressed people. They helped strengthen faith and community and fostered the dream of freedom. Some songs originating from the slavery period had another purpose: they communicated information about the UGGR to slaves through coded messages. Some examples used in this novel are "Follow the Drinking Gourd," "Wade in the Water," "I Couldn't Hear Nobody Pray," and "Steal Away."

As I researched the history of Afro-American song, I discovered a lot of "angel" songs from the days of slavery that mirrored Phoebe's dreams of flying: "Run, Mona, Run"; "I've Got A Robe"; "Toll de Bell Angel, I Just Got Over" and "I Got Two Wings". The title of this novel is based on a line from "Run, Mona, Run". Sources for musical history include: "Wade in the Water," an audio history of Afro-American song as compiled by Dr. Bernice Johnson Regan of the Smithsonian Institute, *Songs of Zion* (Abingdon Press, 1982), *Mellows* by R. Emmet Kennedy (Albert & Charles Boni, 1925), and *Follow the Drinking Gourd* by J. Winter (Dragonfly/Knopf, 1988).

All the routes on the UGRR headed to Canada, or "the promised land," as the slaves called it. Once they reached it, they were protected. Although the United States demanded their return from the British government, Canada refused to release the slaves. More than forty thousand slaves reached safety in Canada but thousands died along the way. Their names will never be known.

Most of the depots that sheltered runaways were located in southwestern Ontario, that part of Canada closest to the United States, easily reached by water. Slaves swam across the Detroit River, their belongings on their back, or sailed like Phoebe across Lake Erie. British abolitionists and clergymen helped to shelter slaves and taught them skills to make a living in Canada. They assisted slaves in building the houses, farms, and schools they would need to form self-sufficient communities.

Today, descendants of runaway slaves still live in southwestern Ontario and preserve the old depots and settlements at the end of the UGRR. You can meet them at the UGRR sites on the African-Canadian Heritage Tour: Buxton National Historical Site in North Buxton, Uncle Tom's Cabin in Dresden, WISH Centre in Chatham, The North American Black Historical Museum in Amherstburg, Sandwich First Baptist Church in Windsor, and also The John Freeman Walls Historic Site in Puce. You can find out more about these sites at www.africanhertour.org.

Dreams are what carry us.
Virginia Frances Schwartz